FLESH GUITAR

Geoff Nicholson was born in Sheffield and went to the Universities of Cambridge and Essex. His novels include *Street Sleeper*, *Hunters and Gatherers*, *Everything and More*, *Footsucker* and *Bleeding London*, which was shortlisted for the Whitbread Award. He has also published two works of non-fiction: *Big Noises* and *Day Trips to the Desert*. His works have been translated into French, German, Japanese, Italian and Polish.

From

A.P. WATT LTD.
20 John Street, London, WC1N 2DR to whom please address all communications about the work to which this slip is attached.

FLESH GUITAR

Geoff Nicholson

VICTOR GOLLANCZ

LONDON

First published in Great Britain 1998
by Victor Gollancz
An imprint of the Cassell Group
Wellington House, 125 Strand, London WC2R 0BB

A Gollancz Paperback Original

A catalogue record for this book is
available from the British Library.

ISBN 0 575 06489 7

Typeset by Rowland Phototypesetting Ltd,
Bury St Edmunds, Suffolk
Printed and bound in Great Britain by
Guernsey Press Co. Ltd, Guernsey, Channel Isles

98 99   5 4 3 2 1

The girl bent over her guitar,
An axeman of sorts. The day was green.

They said, 'You have a flesh guitar,
You do not play things as they are.'

The 'girl' replied, 'Jesus Christ, everybody's
a fucking critic these days. Go and make your
own album if you feel that way about it, why
doncha?'

HAVOC

She throws open the door and walks into an end-of-the-world watering hole called the Havoc Bar and Grill, a converted research laboratory somewhere on the outer fringes of the metropolis. She is carrying a guitar. Its case looks ordinary enough. It is scuffed and well-travelled, her name – JENNY SLADE – is stencilled on the side, and it has a few old stickers for amp and effects manufacturers, but there is nothing about the case that gives any hint of what's inside.

The bar's decor is early post-nuclear holocaust; exposed pipes and ducting, mutilated concrete, buckled metal furniture. The customers might have been specially designed to match. The crowd is male, drunk, aggressive, misogynistic, and adolescent in mind, if not in age. They all lack a certain something: good looks, teeth, fingers, brain cells. Undifferentiated hostility hangs over them like a cloud of swamp gas. Behind the bar a waif-like barmaid does her best to keep the rabble in check, at least while they're ordering their drinks. The badge on her white T-shirt says she's called Kate.

One of the drinkers looks at Jenny Slade and says, 'Hey, the stripper's arrived,' but even he knows it's not a good joke. She doesn't look at all like a stripper. She doesn't look much like a guitar player either. Oh sure, she has the beat-up leather jacket and the motorcycle boots. And she has the cheekbones and the mess of wild hair, but she isn't posing as some kind of guitar heroine. She isn't playing at being tough. She looks strong but not hard-bitten. She looks self-possessed and able to take care of herself, but that hasn't destroyed an essential sensitivity and vulnerability, even a fragility. Jenny looks over her feral audience and smiles. She's played far more difficult rooms than this one.

She can't remember a time when she didn't play the guitar. She was the kind of kid who sat alone in Dad's garage, yanking weird noise out of a plywood cheese-grater guitar. That might have been considered a strange thing for a good-looking teenage girl to be doing, but she had always been far beyond that kind of suburban nonsense.

Even back then she liked to think of herself as a relentless experimentalist. She employed what she only learned later was called 'extended technique'. She could play conventionally enough when the gig required it, but at other times she attacked the guitar with hammers, box spanners, nail guns, adzes, spokeshaves. She would dangle house keys, six-inch nails, rusty razor blades, spark plugs, nipple clamps, from the strings. She loved feedback, distortion, sheer noise. She liked to abuse both guitar and equipment. She knew this wasn't going to get her into the charts but it made her happy, and if it didn't always make her audiences happy that was OK, since for a long time she seldom had an audience.

She orders a beer from the barmaid and props the guitar case against the bar. The manager of the Havoc, a bald, bearded ex-biker, comes over and asks, 'What kind of axe you got in there?'

'It's custom made.'

'Yeah? Can you play it?'

'Yes, thanks,' she says.

'Tell you what,' he says, with what he takes to be a devilish glint in his eyes, 'the beer's on the house if you can get up on the stage and keep my customers entertained for a couple of numbers.'

'Oh, I can do *that*,' she says, and her face says that she can do a lot more besides.

The barman tells her she can plug into an old Brand X ten-watt amplifier, miked into the house PA. He admits it isn't an ideal arrangement, but it's fine by her. She knows that in the end it isn't a matter of equipment.

By now the crowd is taking quite an interest. They're too hip in their malevolence actively to taunt her, but they leave their seats and the pool table, and they crowd in around the bar's tiny stage, their body language challenging her to impress them.

She stands on the stage, looking suddenly much smaller and younger. She still hasn't taken the guitar out of its case, but now she snaps open the clasps. There's a noise like a sigh, and a wisp of what looks like steam, or maybe even hot breath, billows from the case.

She reaches inside and takes out this *thing*. Well yes, you'd have to admit it was a guitar, but none of these drinkers, these lovers of good ol' rock and roll, has ever seen one like this before. The neck is made out of some kind of unnaturally lustrous metal, so shiny it almost has a glow to it. It is long and thick, and convincingly phallic. The strings run along its length, ultra light, ultra malleable, and end at the machine heads in a lethal-looking tangle of spikes and cogs and chains.

But this is the orthodox bit of the guitar. It's the body that defies belief. It is shaped like an amoeba, which is to say that it's curvy but essentially shapeless; and it appears at first glance to be made out of some sort of tan-coloured plastic. But the more you look, the less it appears to be plastic at all. In fact it looks more like a piece of soft, private flesh, and in places there are growths of hair bursting out in thick, black, irregular tufts. There are blemishes that on a piece of wood might look like knots, but here they look disturbingly like nipples, and the pickups look like three parallel bands of livid scar tissue.

'Hey, what do you call that sucker?' someone yells.

'I call it a guitar,' Jenny Slade answers quietly.

She straps it on, this instrument that looks part deadly weapon and part creature from some alien lagoon. She plugs a lead into a deep orifice in the thing's surface, and the bar manager takes the other end of the lead and runs it into the amp.

Without tuning up she grabs the neck at the seventh fret, holds down a fairly straightforward-looking chord, and picks out a lazy arpeggio with her plectrum hand. Well, the guitar isn't in standard tuning, that's for sure. The chord contains all kinds of weird harmonies, unisons, octaves, diminished sevenths, augmented fourths, suspended ninths. In fact it sounds like the richest, most complicated chord anyone has ever heard. And that guitar has absolutely incredible sustain.

She's barely touched the strings and yet the whole room is filled with that dense, ringing, fluid sound. It's not so very loud, yet it demands absolute attention. It isn't a sound you could dance to exactly but it sure keeps you on your feet.

And as the music hangs in the air the guitar tone is not a wholly pleasant sound. It has elements of feedback in it, elements of white noise, of grunge and skronk. And yet it remains listenable and utterly compelling. Nobody's walking out of this performance.

It is a truth universally acknowledged that when somebody comes on stage and makes horrible noise with, say, a saxophone, the audience tends to dismiss the performance as 'just a load of fucking about'. Whereas when somebody comes on stage and makes horrible noise with an electric guitar, the audience is far more likely to say, 'Holy moly! Ruined cities of sonic mayhem! Give me more!' One day Jenny thinks she may come to understand the reason for this, but for now she's happy just to take advantage of the fact.

She might have stayed a bedroom guitarist all her life if it hadn't been for a dream she had. It was the last of a series. Often these dreams were full of frustration; she would be on stage playing an electric guitar in front of an audience and something would always be wrong. Sometimes she couldn't get the guitar in tune, sometimes it was too quiet to be heard, sometimes the lead from the guitar to the amplifier was too short to be usable.

But this final dream was different in several ways. In this one she didn't even get as far as going on stage, and yet there was no frustration. She simply arrived at a strange hall in a strange town and outside was a poster advertising her presence. The poster said, 'The Flesh Guitar of Jenny Slade', and there was a crowd of thousands trying to get into the hall.

She liked the name. Even in the dream it seemed kind of absurd and funny, and she knew how important a catchy name is for entry-level rock musicians. Next day she set about forming a band, Jenny Slade and the Flesh Guitars; and sure enough she did eventually see her name on a poster, and even occasionally saw crowds of people going into a hall.

It was not in the strictest sense a prophetic dream. Yes, it did forecast what was to happen, but only because Jenny *made* it happen. But if she hadn't had the dream perhaps it would never have happened at all.

Mostly her early fantasy life didn't come so directly from the unconscious. Some of it was just playing around in front of a mirror, some of it was just rock and roll teen dreams. She imagined performing under the name of Juanita and Her Musical Snakes. She would come on stage with a Gibson Moderne and half a dozen boa constrictors of various ages, lengths and diameters. The more sedate of these would grip themselves around the guitar neck and hold down unresolved chord shapes, while the younger more slender critters would squirm across the strings creating wild atonal arpeggios. The liveliest snake, whom she nicknamed Fidel, would curl himself around the tremolo arm and create a profound and unworldly vibrato. The audience would love it. But even in the fantasy Jenny was aware that this was just a novelty act, and she wanted more than that.

Another fantasy: If a guitar is cranked up high enough, with the amp, and pickups and fuzz box all sex on maximum, even the slightest vibration, a knock on the body, the mere act of picking up the instrument will produce noise. In one of her earliest, most radical pieces Jenny's playing consisted of no more than blowing on her guitar strings.

In the fantasy she imagines she is in an empty, desolate landscape, strapped into a kind of wheeled electric chair. The wheels fit on to railway tracks, and there is a powerful engine attached to the back of the chair. She is holding a guitar, and it is cranked up so that every breath of wind sets the strings roaring. A wireless transmitter sends signals from the pickups to a mountainous wall of amps and speakers set up some distance away.

When the moment comes, the engine will propel the chair along the railway track, and the rush of air will make the guitar whine; then, when the track runs out, like in some *Roadrunner* cartoon, she will be propelled into space, into a vast, deep canyon, still strapped to the chair, still clutching the guitar. And as she falls through the air the guitar screams and sings, and she knows that when she and guitar eventually hit the ground, the most wild, eloquent and destructive music will issue from the speakers.

And finally there is the fantasy of playing to a crowd of fierce, low-brow, blue-collar yobs; but the Havoc Bar and Grill is all too real, no fantasy at all.

Jenny's guitar continues to fill the place. Her playing remains simple and unostentatious. She hardly seems to be doing anything, scarcely playing at all, and yet this strange, wonderful music continues to spill from the guitar. The music gets ever more complex and darker, gets louder and louder, and before long it seems to be the sound of planets melting, of death factories imploding, of mythical beasts being slaughtered, the sound of air moving and valves dying. It goes on and on, timelessly, constant, yet ever changing.

And as the crowd watches, increasingly spellbound, the guitar seems to develop a life of its own. It seems to be breathing, to be pulsing with its own heartbeat. And then the finale. Just when you can't imagine how Jenny Slade can possibly embellish or prolong the music, and when you can't see how she's ever going to bring it to a conclusion, the guitar starts to bleed. Thick warm blood starts to ooze from the scar tissue of the pickups, trickles down the guitar's body, makes dark, scattered blots on the stage.

It's a hard act to follow. The audience is silent, but gives Jenny what she wants and needs; unqualified, undivided attention. And she takes certain energies away from them. But that's OK, it's not as if they were using those energies for anything much. As forms of vampirism go, this one is relatively benevolent. She brings the music to an end, a long diminuendo, a series of descending melancholy minor chords.

Jenny would always claim that guitar playing has something in common with chaos theory. A simple movement of her plectrum, a pluck of a string, a movement no greater or more dramatic than that of a butterfly's wing, would create a signal which could sound as loud, as complex, as elaborate as the sounds that might accompany the end of the world.

The music starts to evaporate. Smoke and decay and a new silence hang in the air. The customers in the bar are not quite sure what they've heard or seen, but they're suddenly in need, acutely aware that they're dying for a drink. They huddle around the bar, and the barmaid has a hard time coping with their urgent demands for more booze.

Nobody applauds Jenny Slade. It wasn't that kind of performance, but she's well contented with the audience response. She sits down at a corner table and the manager sends over a beer. The crowd are in awe of her, deferential and too shy to approach her. Jenny slips her guitar into its case and snaps its lid shut with a bold, decisive gesture. Done it. It's finished.

Nearby is a young kid, not more than seventeen years old, all Celtic tattoos, multiple piercings, blond hair and dirty denim, a tough cherub. He's alone at a table full of empty beer bottles lined up like ten pins, but he appears sober. When Jenny looks towards him he turns his gaze aside, but he can't ignore her when she says, 'You're a guitar player, aren't you?'

'That's right,' he admits. 'How could you tell?'

'The way you watched me play. The way you twitched your fingers.'

He grins shyly. 'Yeah, I should stop playing air guitar, shouldn't I?'

'I've got something I want to give you,' Jenny says.

He blushes, aware of the sexual innuendo, but he can't respond, and his embarrassment turns to dumb amazement as Jenny Slade hands him her guitar.

'It's all yours,' she says, and she drains her beer and heads for the exit.

'Hey, hey,' the boy says, and he gets up and pursues her

15

out on to the street. All eyes from the bar turn and look out through the grey mottled windows to watch the dumbshow that now takes place; his mimed reluctance to accept the gift, Jenny Slade's absolute refusal to take no for an answer. They watch as finally Jenny walks away and the boy doesn't follow her. The guitar is his, though he has no idea what future comes with it. He is too stunned to return to the bar, and he too wanders off into the night, guitar in hand, but in the opposite direction from Jenny.

'What was that all about?' Kate the barmaid asks. 'Of all the juke joints in all the world, why here? What did she want?'

None of the drinkers offers an answer; they've already got enough to think about. That was quite some cabaret turn they just witnessed. They finish their beers and slowly start to drift away. The manager talks of closing early, and Kate begins cleaning up the bar and stacking some of the chairs.

At which point the door of the bar is thrown open again. This time it's a plump, uncool lad in a tangle of thick, ill-fitting clothes, laden down with several carrier bags, a brief-case, a rucksack. Greasy hair is tucked in behind his ears and his face shows the trouble he's having breathing. He's panting like a greyhound and the sweat pours down the sides of his nose, letting his horn-rims slip so that he peers over the top of them. He's exactly the kind of nerd the bar's clientele would normally have a lot of fun taking apart. He speaks only with great effort.

'Am I too late?' he asks of the almost empty room.

Nobody responds and he hustles up to the bar. The

manager ignores him completely and the barmaid carries on with her stacking, but eventually she calls across the room to ask what he wants.

'Did I miss Jenny Slade?' he asks, but something in his voice shows that he already knows the answer.

'Was that her name?' Kate replies. 'Yeah, you missed a good show.'

'A good show,' he repeats bleakly.

'Actually,' she says, 'it was more than a good show. It was a great show, totally cool. I was completely blown away.'

He slams his fist down on the bar and for a moment it looks as though he's going to do the same thing with his head. There are tears in his eyes, tears of pain and absolute despair.

'Can I get you a drink?' Kate asks sympathetically.

'Yes, whisky, lots of it.'

She eyes him uncertainly. He's young, doesn't look as though he's much of a drinker, but he definitely needs something to sustain and console him.

'Water with that?' she enquires.

He doesn't reply so she dilutes the whisky with a good splash of water. She doesn't know why she should care. She sees young men drink themselves into oblivion every night of the week, but there does seem to be something uniquely vulnerable about this guy.

'Come far?' she asks.

'From the ends of the earth.'

'Yeah, you really missed something special,' Kate says.

'I know,' he yells. 'I KNOW THAT!'

The manager glances over, wondering if the guy's a

troublemaker in need of bouncing, but he seems harmless enough and Kate is a much tougher cookie than she looks. The new arrival takes off his spectacles and lets the sweat and tears run freely down his wide, rounded cheeks.

'Please tell me about it,' he sobs.

'What?'

'Describe Jenny Slade's performance to me. Please.'

The barmaid tries but it isn't easy. She can't put her enthusiasm into words, can't begin to express the excitement of it. Besides, he wants masses of detail, more than she can provide. She wasn't all that aware, for instance, of how Jenny Slade was dressed or how she stood or what the piece of music was, or what gauge of string she was using. Kate just knows that she loved it. Her account is lively but it does nothing to enliven the new customer. The more she enthuses, the more miserable he becomes.

'What's your name anyway?' she asks.

'Bob,' he says. 'Bob Arnold, and I'm Jenny Slade's number one fan.'

'Is that right?'

'Yes, it is.'

'Well, you have very good taste. So how come I never heard of her before?'

'Because she's a cult,' Bob says shortly.

'Tell me more.'

'How long have you got?'

Kate thinks of the cheap, cold, low-ceilinged room that she calls home, a place she doesn't want to return to. Then she contemplates a bar full of drink, the offer of company and the chance to hear more about Jenny Slade, though admittedly from a guy who looks like a nerd, and she replies encouragingly, 'I've got as long as it takes.'

A PUTATIVE EARLY LIFE

We can try to imagine Jenny Slade's childhood; unhappy and solitary is always best for an artist. Did she come from conventional if progressive parents who encouraged their daughter in everything she did? Or was her mother a drunk, her father violent when not absent? And did some uncle encourage her to play music, did he pooh-pooh the notion that there was anything wrong with a thirteen-year-old girl strapping on an electric guitar? Did he go with her to buy her first good instrument, tune it for her, teach her some chords, pay for a few lessons?

What was her guitar teacher like? An ageing, chain-smoking rocker maybe, with a Ritchie Blackmore fixation, who after six months said, 'Go, I can teach you no more'?

Did he like to talk about it afterwards?

'Oh, I couldn't really pretend that I taught Jenny Slade how to play the guitar,' he might say, all appropriately modest. 'With someone like Jenny that's not what happens. You just show them how to start playing, how to start *learning* to play, and then you stand back and watch as they take off on that big, wide learning curve.

'You know, there's a certain kind of student whose hands

just seem to curl naturally around the neck of the guitar and land on the fingerboard in just the right places. Jenny was like that.'

And does he shake his head a little sadly, savouring a sweet sorrow, as he says, 'But one thing I've learned in my long teaching career is that it's not about fingers. Fingers are finite whereas the human spirit is infinite. So it makes sense to play guitar with your spirit rather than your digits.

'And one more thing I'll say; start a girl or boy playing the guitar and they've got a metaphor *of* life and *for* life.'

And did she read Bert Weedon's *Play in a Day*, and did she abandon it because she wasn't sure she really wanted to know how to play 'Bobby Shafto'?

Did she play rhythm guitar for her older brother and his friends, creating a backing for their long, inept solos? Did the arrangement come to an end, not because Jenny was bored with her role (in fact regarding it as some sort of Zen discipline) but because the boys realized she had outgrown them?

Did she walk into guitar shops, those complex arenas of male intimidation, and refuse to be intimidated? Did she overhear the salesman say, 'Y'know as a guy gets older his dick seems to recede more and more – maybe it's something to do with the size of his gut; anyways, when you hit middle age you're generally in need of a little symbolic phallic extension. Some guys buy a Corvette, me, I recommend this lil' beaut.

'It's called the Splatocaster. Pretty as a penis, ten times as big. Show your woman the spec on this monster and she'll

21

be squealing like a teeny bopper. She'll be crying out for an encore and you'll be able to give it to her.'

Did he only say all that stuff to embarrass her? Did she have to overcome sexist abuse? Did people tell her she needed balls to play the guitar? Did they say she played pretty good *for a chick*? Did she think Angus Young was a sad little fuck when he said that his ideal guitar would be a 'cannon that shot sperm at the audience'? Or did she think he was a supreme ironist?

Did she have heroines? Did she dote on Ari Up and Ivy Rorschach and Sister Rosetta Tharpe, or was it less gender specific than that? Was it Bowie and Ronson, the rock performer as androgyne? We can assume a tortured adolescence. She was nobody's idea of a dream date. She stayed in her room, read poetry, practised her guitar, listened to Django Reinhardt and Eddie Van Halen and Gaye Advert.

We can take for granted the false starts, the rip-offs, the broken promises, the bands that broke up after one gig, the managers who could make her a star. The rest we have to imagine, although there is the following rather improbable text that appeared in the fanzine *JOSS* (*The Journal of Sladean Studies*), a piece purporting to be about Jenny Slade's early experiences on the road. It is generally assumed that Jenny Slade did not in fact write the words, that the piece is fictionalized 'autobiography', written by a third party. Yet Jenny never objected to the publication and subsequent anthologizing of the piece so we assume she must have thought that in some sense it contains the truth about her early days on the road.

DICK

Call me Jenny Slade. Some years ago, having little or no money, and nothing particular to interest me at home, I thought I would tour about a little and see the rock and roll parts of the world. It is a way I have of driving off the blues. Whenever I find myself playing exclusively minor chords, when I find myself listening to Leonard Cohen albums, when it requires a strong act of will to prevent me from braining promoters, record reviewers and teeny boppers with the blunt end of my guitar, then I account it high time to get on the road as soon as I can.

I found myself signed up as rhythm guitarist with an outfit called Captain Ahab and His Magic Big Band, an intermittently outrageous combo with its roots in the blues. The eponymous Captain, originally just plain Johnny Ahab, sang, played harmonica and sometimes shouted a sort of cracked, surreal poetry. I knew the tour would be a learning experience, and would look good on my CV, even if the good Captain himself had a reputation for being difficult to work and live with. I thought I could handle him, but I didn't know the half of it.

It was going to be a long, arduous world tour calling in at the Azores, Rio de la Plata, Sumatra, Java; all the hot spots. And the band was hot too. On bass there was the very heavy and very tattooed Sam Queequeg. He looked fearsome, but he was a great man to have on your side; certainly if somebody tried to invade the stage. Playing keyboards and acting as musical director was Randy Starbuck, the Captain's right-hand man from way back. Billy Stubb was the drummer, and he was supplemented by Rikki Tashtego, a percussionist and the Native American of the group.

Each of them was a musical giant in his own right and they had all led their own bands at one time or another, but it was clear that on this particular tour they would be subservient to the genius and obsessive vision of the Captain.

It was some time before I met the man himself. I was auditioned and recruited by Randy Starbuck alone. The Captain would only show up when we were fully drilled and rehearsed. We had to be tight, disciplined and controlled so that we could become his creatures, and give him the freedom to pursue his own strange, lofty goals. What these goals were we only slowly discovered.

We were put through our paces in an old, disused whaling station in Nantucket, and although the Captain was rumoured to be in town we weren't allowed to see him. His absence had a strange effect on the band. We all felt apprehensive and uneasy. We already suspected that the rehearsals would scarcely prepare us for the task ahead. We played as well as we could and yet we knew it would all be totally different the moment the tour started.

It was not until we'd been playing together for two weeks or more that the Captain finally put in an appearance. Starbuck had led us through a beefy, somewhat shambolic instrumental version of Rod Stewart's 'Sailing', which had ended in a loose but undeniably exciting burst of improvised sound and fury. We looked up and there was the Captain, standing at the back of the hall.

He was quite a spectacle. There seemed no sign of common bodily illness. His whole high, broad form seemed made of solid bronze and shaped in an unalterable mould like Cellini's cast of Perseus or like an Oscar statuette. He was wintry, bare, rugged, like a thunder-cloven oak.

He had a formidable scar. It started high up in his long grey hair, continued white and livid down one side of his tanned, chiselled face and neck, and disappeared inside the collar of his black silk shirt. Whether he was born with the scar, or whether it was the result of over-enthusiastic audience participation on some earlier tour, I couldn't say, but by mutual consent it was never mentioned by anyone.

So charismatic was the Captain that at first I hardly noticed the curious false leg on which he stood. How he had lost his real leg I had no idea at the time, but I could see it had been replaced by a false one fashioned from the rosewood neck of a pre-CBS Fender Telecaster. It gave him a strange, insecure posture, not entirely unlike Gene Vincent. You couldn't look away. When he shambled on to the stage, any stage, and hooked that leg around the microphone stand and began to sing, people took notice. Snappier critics than I have written that he 'had crucifixion in his face and all the regal, overbearing dignity of some mighty woe', and I couldn't put it better myself.

We went through 'Sailing' again. The Captain sang a couple of verses with us. His sudden appearance had thrown us into musical confusion. We played extremely badly for him, and yet when he got to the end of the song, as the band crashed hopelessly out of time, and into a chaos of discord and disharmony, an expression came upon his face that in other men might have resulted in a smile. We knew then that this was going to be a tour to remember.

We began in earnest. The tour was long and hard. The hotels were cheap and cheerless, the travel arrangements chaotic. We ate too little and drank too much. Drugs were popped at every conceivable occasion. Such sex as was encountered was brief and animalistic. It was just another tour in those respects. But, if I say so myself, the music was pretty good, and we were glad about that. We all wanted to do a good job for the Captain. Yet at the same time I think we were also aware that we might never quite be able to live up to the standards he was setting.

And as we toured we heard stories and rumours about the Captain, and though many of them were absurd or downright contradictory, they gradually gelled and made sense. We realized soon enough the nature of his mission. Quite simply he was in search of the Great White Noise. He had heard it once, had indeed created it with an early incarnation of the Big Band. It all stemmed from a date in a gaucho bar in Patagonia. It had started like an ordinary gig, but as the evening progressed the music had become increasingly free-form, increasingly wild. The band was blowing up a storm, something supernatural and terrifying. They played on for hours, rode the whirlwind till they feared for their very souls. A point came when they were no longer playing music, rather they were involved in something perilous and incorporate and life-threatening. It was indeed a great white noise that drew them to the edge of madness and mayhem.

They played till they couldn't play any more, until they were spent and all the music had been wrung out of them. When they eventually left the stage they were wrecked, but they all thought it was worth it for the sake of having produced that wild, wild noise.

However, it turned out to be a one-off, an end rather than a beginning, a fluke perhaps. They were never able to recapture that sound, that moment, and so the Captain broke up the band, decided to try again from scratch. From then on he had toured the world, his monomania heavy upon him, always trying out new bands, new equipment, seeking out new audiences and venues. He'd hear of a hot new bass player from Estonia, of a happening club in Mauritania, and he would be there trying to recreate that sound; but to date he had failed miserably. Consequently his manner was both frantic and morbid, and it seemed to us that he put into his quest all the general rage and hate felt by his whole race from Adam down.

And we also heard stories of how he came to lose his leg. It was said that on that famous occasion he was so transported by the music, so utterly delirious, that he climbed to the top of a stack of speakers and fell off, shattering his leg. Despite all the administrations of a good Patagonian surgeon, the leg was lost, and in the madness of his convalescence he decreed that he would become a living instrument, the means by which that great white noise was recaptured, hence the neck of the Telecaster. It sounded like far-fetched stuff, yet nobody who met the Captain had any trouble believing it.

We toured on. There were good gigs and bad gigs. Gigs when we didn't play as well as we wanted to, gigs where we played supremely well. But the only gigs that interested the Captain were those where a kind of madness came over us, when we played beyond ourselves, when we successfully pushed and tore the envelope. Some audiences seemed to understand what we were about and urged us on, others simply found us crazed and incomprehensible.

The Captain was enough of an old pro that he could never be accused of shortchanging an audience, but he didn't see himself simply as an entertainer. He was going all the way and if the audience couldn't go with him that was just too bad. There were nights when we thought we were getting close, when the music was pure abstraction, something radical and deranged, but the Captain insisted we go further. Within the band there were those who suspected it might all end in tears, that the Captain might lead us into some sort of rock and roll hell from which there was no return, but nobody ever suggested we hold back or try to pace ourselves. Maybe it was the drugs, maybe it was exhaustion, but we were all prepared to follow him to the end of the line.

And so we came at last to Tierra del Fuego, the final stretch of the tour, back to those regions where the Captain had first encountered his white noise and lost a part of himself. It had been a very long tour. We were infinitely weary. All the humour and joy seemed to have been forced out of us and yet we played on. The Captain had driven us to the ends of our tether, till we were in a state of such spiritual malaise that we were nothing more than his pawns, his playthings. Dumbly we moved through the sound check, ever conscious of the old man's despot eye, aware that he was willing us to bring the tour to a dramatic, shattering conclusion.

The gig started in front of a big enthusiastic audience, and the Captain led us into a version of 'Ferry Cross The Mersey', a version such as you've never heard. It was as though he were playing for his very life, for all our lives. If the Captain was aware of his surroundings, of the club we were in, of the way the audience responded, he failed to show it. His gaze was fixed upon dim and distant horizons and he sang and played like a man possessed.

The band playing on, rolling and swaying. Sometimes the music shuddered and splintered, as though threatening to fall apart, and yet somehow we continued. The Captain played his harmonica for all he was worth. 'There he blows,' Sam Queequeg shouted over and over again, really getting off on the awesome beauty of the noise. The Captain drove us on. We played faster and faster, skimming over melodies, re-forming them so that they flowed and rippled, were turned to surf and waves, until at last a moment came when we no longer knew what we were playing. Tonight was going to be the night. We had gone beyond technique, beyond conscious intention. We were maniacs. It was all wind rush and spume, and it was truly magnificent. We were lost, utterly lost, at the mercy of forces much greater than ourselves. But there it was. We knew we had finally succeeded in creating the great white noise that the Captain had been pushing us so hard to locate.

'At last,' he said between atonal blasts on his mouth harp. 'At last.'

He stood rooted in front of the microphone as if he were no longer with us, his mind transported to some dim, blue, vacant place. The audience went crazy. They pressed against the stage like a flood tide, and the Captain leaned towards them, reached out, tilted perilously in their direction, trusting them, wanting to become one with them, to float upon the sea of people.

He launched himself. It was a terrible mistake. Stage diving was entirely unknown in that part of the world. The welcoming

29

supporting raised hands he had been expecting were not there for him. Instead a gap opened up in the crowd and the bare floor of the hall became visible. The Captain plunged downwards, hit the deck with a horrifying crack, and helplessly he yielded to his body's doom. Then the crowd closed in around him and he disappeared like one trodden underfoot by herds of stampeding polo ponies. Nameless wails came from him, as desolate sounds from far ravines. There was a terrible beauty in knowing that these sounds were unlikely ever to be repeated.

The band stopped playing, but the audience scarcely noticed. They were mad now, as mad as we members of the band had been, as mad as the Captain. We had created in them a frenzy that we could not possibly control. What's more, we were now leaderless and redundant. We decided to make a dash for it. We ran from the stage and in the process lost almost everything we had, our instruments, our amplifiers, our PA system. The audience wrecked the hall, the dressing rooms, our tour bus. Security guards muscled in, started cracking heads and waving baseball bats around. The gig was over, and so was the tour, and so was a whole phase of my life. Perhaps it was because I was a woman that I alone survived unharmed to tell the tale.

Reprinted from the *Journal of Sladean Studies*
Volume 5 Issue 8

MEANWHILE BACK AT THE BAR

'Frankly,' says Kate, the barmaid at the Havoc Bar and Grill, 'I've never really understood what the big deal is about the electric guitar.'

Bob Arnold looks as though she has stabbed him in the heart.

'Well, thanks for being frank,' he says bleakly.

She has provided him with his second drink, poured something for herself, and the two of them are sitting in a pale cone of light at the corner of the bar, while around them other drinkers settle into snoring, lumpen stupors, and the manager contemplates going home and leaving Kate to lock up.

'Well,' says Bob wearily, but with patience, as though he's explained all this stuff a million times before but still thinks it worthwhile to explain it again, 'the thing is: the electric guitar is a conduit. It connects with pain and passion, with inspiration and aspiration, with sound waves and electrical charge, with technology and history, with industry and the heart.'

'Oh,' says Kate, strikingly aware that she may be out of her depth here, or more specifically that she has fallen into conversation with a serious guitar bore. He wouldn't be the first to have bent her ear. However, Bob's take on things seems a little more interesting than those she's suffered through before.

He says, 'The electric guitar is a strange combination of electronics and mechanics. The simple movement of the fingers is translated by electricity into sound.

'An electric guitar has pickups. The pickup consists of a magnet or magnetic pole pieces surrounded by a wire coil. When a steel string vibrates within the magnetic field it induces a current in the coil. That electric signal is sent out of the guitar along a lead to an amp and speakers. Jenny Slade and I always like to think it has something in common with chaos theory, but I won't trouble you with that now.'

'Thanks,' says Kate.

He continues. 'The unamplified acoustic guitar has always been a rather quiet, impotent sort of thing. It was OK for folk singers or country blues singers, or even to accompany flamenco dancers, but put it up against a full jazz band or the Benny Goodman Orchestra and it becomes pretty well inaudible. So it needed to be louder.

'There's a lot of infighting about who invented the electric guitar; Lloyd Loar at Gibson was in with a claim, the guys at Dobro too, but the fact is, nothing much predates the Frying Pan.'

'Excuse me?' says Kate.

'It was a nineteen thirty-one prototype; a long thin guitar neck with a solid circular body, hence the Frying Pan. Arnold Rickenbacker, George Beauchamp, an assistant called Paul Barth, a guitar-maker called Harry Watson, they all had a hand in creating it. It's said that Beauchamp began by taking the pickup from a Brunswick phonograph and attaching it to a piece of two-by-four with a single string. The pickup translated the vibration of the string and amplified it. Adding five more strings and giving the guitar a more conventional shape was just icing on the cake. The basic principle had been established.

'By nineteen thirty-two Rickenbacker was manufacturing the Electro Spanish guitar, a perfectly modern looking piece of gear with f holes and fancy volume and tone controls, but the pickup is exactly like on the Frying Pan.'

Bob is aware that some of this may be a little technical for his listener, but she did ask for it, and he would never dream of talking down to a person just because she worked behind a bar. And besides it's so much easier to talk about history and technology than it is to talk about what's really breaking his heart.

'Anyway,' Bob says, 'being the first is nice, but it isn't everything. Some things are simply inevitable. If Beauchamp hadn't come up with the Frying Pan somebody else would have.

'Leo Fender was the first to mass-produce electric guitars. He made 'em cheap and he made 'em good. And if he hadn't started producing them, then Gibson certainly wouldn't have set up in competition, in which case Les Paul would never have been called in and the whole history of the electric guitar would have been different.

'But note that I only say *different*. If Fender hadn't been the Henry Ford of guitars, somebody else would have been. If Les Paul hadn't invented that fat, eloquent humbucking sound, somebody else would. These things were simply bound to happen.

'And after those few basic but crucial inventions, after those patents and practices, it didn't really matter. After that, the deluge. After that there came tens of thousands of designers and inventors, craftsman and manufacturers, customizers and luthiers, all trying to "reinvent" the electric guitar. But basically they were all too late. The job had been done and the party was over. The rest was just tidying and sweeping up.'

'You certainly know your history,' Kate says.

'Those who don't know history are doomed to do bad cover versions,' he quips. 'Now, there's a reasonable argument that says the best electric guitars are the biggest failures. You see, the pioneers of the electric guitar wanted a device that could reproduce the sound of an acoustic guitar as accurately and with as pure a tone as possible, so that it sounded exactly like an acoustic guitar only louder. But electric guitars never quite do that. They add muck and growl and distortion. And the strange thing is, people discovered they preferred it that way.'

Kate's face shows confusion. She says, 'Why would people prefer muck and growl and distortion to accuracy and purity?'

'People are funny like that, Kate.'

Kate shakes her head sadly.

'And that's why they like effects too.'

'Effects? As in special effects?'

'In a way, yes. If people liked a fuzzy signal, why not make a little machine that could create fuzz to order? And chorus. And phase. And tremolo. And echo. And chorus. And so on and so on.'

'The more the merrier,' Kate adds glibly.

'Frankly, merriness is not one of the things I've ever really looked for in music,' says Bob. 'But yes, when it comes to guitar noise, less is generally not better. Jenny Slade may be many things but she's never been much of a minimalist.'

Kate considers this proposition and finds some truth in it.

'The other element in all this is the amp,' says Bob. 'The guitar and the pickup and the effects units create and modify the signal, and then the amplifier messes it all up some more in its own special way, and cranks it out at skull-crushing volume.'

'And people like that even more?' Kate asks.

'Yes, Kate, some people really like that a lot, believe me.'

'Yes, I'll buy that,' says Kate. 'Jenny Slade's performance wouldn't have been the same if it had been quiet.'

'Look, Kate, here's the true juice,' Bob announces. 'You can quote me on this. Life is like a guitar solo. It's loud, shapeless and it goes on too long. Sometimes it's tuneless, sometimes it's clichéd, either way it's damned difficult to get it right, and even if you've done your best and you're pleased with what you've achieved, you can be sure a lot of people are going to hate it and dump all over you and tell you you're a loser.'

'Aren't *you* the philosopher?' Kate says, not unkindly. 'Do I really need to know all this background just to be able to appreciate Jenny Slade's music?'

'Yes, Kate, you do. Because once you know and understand the background you'll see that the whole of history, of invention, of technical and artistic development, has existed for one reason and one reason only; to bring Jenny Slade to us.'

'Whew,' says Kate, 'that's heavy.' And she reaches for a drink.

'Heavy is the word,' Bob agrees, and he holds out his empty glass so that Kate can refill it.

THE JENNY SLADE INTERVIEW

Bob Arnold chews the fat with Jenny Slade

Jenny Slade was looking especially good when I caught up with her in LA's favourite watering hole, the Giant Anaconda Room. Her look was fearlessly eclectic: the bondage pants, the boob tube, the bolero jacket, the leopardskin pork pie hat, all creating a striking, provocatively sexual image that few could carry off. And yet why did I feel that these fine feathers were hiding a deep hurt? She might have looked like a major babe, but it seemed to me that she was blubbing inside.

I started with a lively and provocative question. 'What happened to all your money, Jenny?'

'Did I ever have any?' she replied wearily. 'Well, maybe I did. I don't know where it went. I guess I spent it all on cheap boys and expensive guitars. Or perhaps it was the other way round; cheap guitars and expensive boys. I forget. Either way, I was never in it for the money, which I agree is perhaps just as well.'

'And how long have you been playing the guitar?'

'For about the same amount of time that the guitar's been playing me,' she quipped gaily, and I got the sense that here was one lady who wasn't going to betray her age.

'I think of you as a true radical,' I said, getting bolder now. 'Always out of step but never out of touch.'

'Are you trying to say that I do not grow old as those who are left grow old?' she intoned.

'I think I'm trying to say that you have a different relationship to the space/time continuum than the rest of us poor mortals.'

'Hmm,' said Jenny, more seriously. 'I will say this: as I get older the appetite for drink and drugs and untrustworthy boys recedes, but the urge to pick up an electric guitar and make a godawful noise just won't go away.'

'And would you say the guitar is a hard instrument to play?' I quizzed provocatively.

She looked at me glancingly, and I knew there was going to be iron *and* irony in her reply.

'Of course it is,' she said. 'If it was easy people like you would be doing it.'

I knew she meant it kindly and we laughed together like old buddies.

'And who are your influences?' I asked.

It was a corny old question but I knew Jenny would come up with a lively and original reply.

She thought for only a moment before replying, 'Willa Cather, Margaret of Anjou, Lady Mary Wortley Montagu, Pamela Des Barres, those sort of people,' and with that she grinned girlishly.

'Do you feel in touch with the modern world?' I challenged.

'I feel in touch with Charlie Christian and Eddie Durham,' she said. 'With Muddy Waters and Chuck Berry and Hank Marvin and Duane Eddy, with Beck and Page and Clapton. With Guitar Slim and Johnny "Guitar" Watson and Clarence "Gatemouth" Brown. With Henry Kaiser and Bernard Butler and Noel Gallagher and Vernon Reid and Winged Eel Fingerling. Sexy fellers, every last one of them. And I feel in touch with women too – though in a different way.

'But mostly I feel in touch with all those lonely boys of the future, still sitting in their rooms trying to play guitar, solemnly believing that if only they could coax some music out of the damn machine they're holding then somehow everything would be better, everything would fall into place; their sex lives, their shyness, their bad skin. And you know what, fellers, you're absolutely right, it would.'

There was a poignant pause while she let that remark settle in.

'You know,' she added briskly, 'it's a long time ago that I decided to be my own woman, my own musician. I decided I was going to tear up the rule book, and then I realized there *was* no rule book.'

I smiled appreciatively but at last I thought it was time to end this verbal jousting. I looked her straight in the eyes and I said, 'Who do you play for, Ms Slade? Yourself or others?'

Arching one carefully plucked eyebrow, she said, 'I play for the nice guys, the filing clerks and computer nerds, the deceived and exploited, for the dysfunctional and the confused and the just plain wrong, for those who are unsure about their identities, their body politics, their genders.

'I play for the decontamination squads, for the firework scientists, the mutants and sleepers. I play for the homely girls terrified by their first sight of menstrual blood, and for the sad boys suffering the attentions of their mothers' special friends. I play for the number crunchers and the atom splitters, for the deformed and the brain dead, for the emotionally drained, for the synaesthesiacs (they make terrific listeners). I play for germ warfare enthusiasts, for the genetic goofballs, the Apple mystics, the road whores, the insurrection grrrls, the nylon broads, the fishnet lads. I often play for the tone deaf.

'I play for those with extra senses and extra heads, for the bad mothers and the cheerful patricides, for the wreckers and the recyclers, the scanners and cyberniks, the video jerks, the steeplejacks of middle space, the boys in the bunker, the hyper-drive cadets, the ovary barons, the born-again crucifiers, the twang bar princesses, the wah wah dudes, the radon lovers, feedback addicts, fuzz theorists.

'I play for the cryogenic fetishists, the orgone punks, the cosmetic surgeons with the shaky hands, the thrash throngs, the synth siblings, the napalm fanciers, the nuclear Klansmen, needlegun gangs, anarchs of the old school, neurone handymen, death metal alchemists.

'I play for the people next door. I play for people like us. I play for people like you, Bob.'

It was a tender and touching moment, but of course she was only telling me what I already knew.

Reprinted from the *Journal of Sladean Studies*
Volume 4 Issue 3

LAST NIGHT I WRECKED A DJ'S LIFE

Jenny Slade could no longer remember which magazine had first referred to Jed Rhodes as a 'drug-crazed bass player'. The epithet had stuck, but she'd always found it absurd. There was no denying that Jed had a lifelong appetite for, maybe even a lifelong love affair with drugs, but it seemed to her there was nothing even remotely crazed about him. He played bass, he took drugs and he remained an utterly sane, rational, ordinary individual. There were times when he became rather quiet and introspective, other times when he might see and talk to things or people or monsters that weren't actually there, but these were small, forgivable eccentricities. The basic, down-to-earth personality always remained. His sense of rhythm never faltered and he never played a bum note.

Jenny sometimes thought Jed didn't deserve to look so good, so healthy, shouldn't be such a walking advertisement for the joys, or at least the essential harmlessness, of drug abuse, but it was an aesthetic judgement not a moral one.

'Drug abuse!' Jed would sneer. 'That's such a pathetic term. What can you do with drugs except abuse them? That's what drugs are *for*.' He'd spent a lifetime just saying yes and he'd done fine, but Jenny knew he was lucky. It wasn't always like that. Few people in the world had the constitution, the inner or outer strength that Jed had, and she certainly did not include herself in that number.

So when she ran into Jed Rhodes in the car-park of a club that was being held in a converted pasta factory just outside the M25 and he offered her an untried and untested chemical, her first reaction was not necessarily to knock it back without hesitation. She also saw that Jed was not alone. He was with a curious young man: a wire-thin, jumpy, wasted-looking, top-of-the-class-in-science type.

'This is Tubby Moran,' Jed said. 'We call him Tubby because he's not. That's drug humour for you. Tubby designs designer drugs, like this one.'

Jed held up a phial about the size of a chemistry lab test tube containing a baby-pink liquid. Tubby Moran looked at the tube and swelled with pride.

'What drug is it?' Jenny asked.

'We call it "Bliss",' Jed replied.

'That's such a dodgy name for a drug,' Jenny said, and she noticed that Tubby looked hurt.

'What's in a name,' Jed insisted. 'It's good. I've taken gallons of the stuff.'

He waved the phial again. The contents certainly looked cute and harmless enough.

'What does it do to you?' she asked.

'Better if I don't tell you,' Jed said. 'That way it's a surprise.'

'Oh, come on!' she protested.

'I promise you it's not harmful, it's not going to make you

believe you can fly or want to have sex with the first eighteen truck drivers you meet.'

'I promise too,' Tubby added reassuringly.

Jed put the phial to his lips and drained a good half of the pink liquid. 'Last chance,' he said, and made as though he was going to swig the rest.

'Oh, all right, damn it,' Jenny said. 'But you're sure I'll like it?'

The two men nodded enthusiastically and Jenny drank half of the remaining dose. Keeping up with Jed's intake was not a game she intended to play. She handed the phial back to him, expecting him to pass it on to Tubby, but he finished the rest himself and the designer-drug boy didn't complain.

'You feel OK?' Jed asked.

'I feel fine, no different.'

'Good. Wait till we get into the club.'

Two bouncers, broad as air-raid shelters, waved them into the club. They looked dubiously at the tragically unhip Tubby Moran, but being with Jed Rhodes was passport enough. They made for the bar.

'Is it OK to drink on top of this stuff?' Jenny asked.

Tubby assured her that it was. As they stood in the crush trying to get served, Jenny became aware of the music. It was something she'd never heard before, a techno beat, a black woman warbling in a high register, not the sort of stuff she normally listened to or liked, yet tonight in the context of the club it sounded really good. And before long she couldn't be bothered to fight her way to the bar; she just wanted to get on the dance floor and immerse herself in the music. Jed followed her and they danced together briefly, but she didn't really notice him. She was dancing with and for herself.

The sound system was fantastic and Jenny took up position next to a speaker, felt the bass and drums ripple through her body. It was truly great. What was this music? It was wonderful, absolutely wonderful. She wanted it to go on forever, she wanted to swim in it, drown in it. And then suddenly a guitar kicked in, digitally enhanced no doubt, sampled and sequenced probably, but it was so perfectly done, so fully on the money, that it hit her like a hammer. But maybe the hammer simile wasn't quite right, maybe it was more like a landslide, an earthquake, a shifting of tectonic plates that cut the ground from under her and let her drop towards the centre of the earth. Jesus, this was a band she'd like to play in.

She didn't know how long the track went on for, but suddenly it was over; it stopped and some other music started to play. Jenny was desolate, and furious as well. What was this crap they'd put on? Why did they take off the good stuff, the great stuff? How could they? She pushed her way through the crowd and found the DJ at his console.

'What was that you were playing?' she demanded.

He named a title and artist that meant nothing to her.

'It was fantastic,' she said. 'Play it again.'

'I just played it.'

'Play it again.'

'Later,' he said.

'Now,' she corrected him. 'Right now.' And she grabbed him by the neck. Her fingers tightened around his windpipe; they were strong fingers – all those years of stretching and dexterity exercises hadn't been wasted – and the DJ's eyes started to pop and he was nodding, OK, OK, he'd play the music again.

Jenny was thrilled and relieved. She really felt something terrible might have happened to her if she'd been deprived of that music for another second, and then she said to herself, 'Oh no. Oh fuck. So *that*'s what the drug does.'

Not that knowing made any difference. As the music returned it took possession of her again, just the way it had before, and the feeling was indeed blissful. Not bad; at last a drug that lived up to its name. She danced on, transported, transformed. Jed had disappeared, Tubby Moran too. No doubt they were blissing out somewhere just like her, but she didn't really care. All that mattered was the music and her engagement with it and that totally amazing guitar sound.

Everything was fine until the music stopped again and the fury came back on her and she launched a second attack on the poor DJ. This time, however, he was prepared. Four bouncers were in place to protect him. It made little difference to Jenny in her present state. She was ready to fight all four of them simultaneously if that's what it took to get the music back. And fight them she did, but it was inevitably a losing battle. Half a minute later she was carried out through the emergency exit and dumped on the tarmac of the car-park. The bouncers re-entered the club and the door slammed shut behind them. Jenny threw herself at the smooth, handleless door, clawed it with her nails, anything to get back to that music.

'Hey kid, you seem to be having what I'd have to call an extreme reaction there.'

She turned to see Jed Rhodes and Tubby Moran trotting up beside her. She scarcely seemed to recognize them, but she did see that Jed was holding a CD.

'It's OK,' he said, trying to calm her. 'I've got the music right here. The DJ was happy to get rid of it. There's a player in my car. You're going to be fine.'

The promise of renewed Bliss was almost too much for her. She thought she might lose control of her mind or her sphincters, but between them Jed and Tubby succeeded in holding her down long enough to strap her into the passenger seat of the car and put the CD in the player and, once again, Jenny returned to her blissful state. Of course, it was only one track on the CD that had the required effect, so Jed pressed the endless replay button and reckoned Jenny was going to be stable, if out of action, for the next few hours.

'Back to the drawing board, eh Tubby?'

'A little redesigning may be required,' Tubby admitted. 'A few small tweaks in the chemical structure are probably all that's needed.'

He left and Jed did his best with Jenny. He felt a sense of responsibility towards her, so he got in the car and drove her home with him. For a long time he sat with her but when she finally appeared to be asleep he decided it was safe to leave her while he went to his own bed. He turned off the music but pressed the CD into her hand so she'd have it if she woke up next morning with the need and the mania still on her.

Fortunately she didn't. Tomorrow was another day. She woke, found herself in the passenger seat, couldn't quite remember what she was doing there, why there was this CD in her hand. But she looked around, realized she was parked in Jed's street, and gradually put two and two together. She made her way to Jed's flat and over coffee and cigarettes she learned a little more about Tubby and Bliss.

'It's early days but I think he's on to something,' Jed insisted. 'Each batch is slightly different, and of course the effects vary with different metabolisms. But basically it means that whatever music you happen to hear when you're on the drug you think it's the best music you've ever heard in your life. Usually you know it's illusory because the music changes and with every change you still think it's the best. Getting hooked on one piece like you did, I've never seen that before. I wonder what would happen if you heard it now.'

Before she could protest Jed had taken the CD from her and put it into a boogie box, and the music was playing again and Jenny steeled herself for the worst and the best. But nothing happened. All she heard was a rather ordinary piece of techno dance music. It moved along OK but it was nothing special, and when the sampled guitar started, well, it was a nice enough piece of sampled guitar, but that was all. She and Jed shared a sigh of relief.

Jenny sipped her coffee. In the cold light of day it all seemed pretty funny, absurd, and given how wonderfully good it had been at the time there were surprisingly few side effects. She felt a little tired and washed out but there was no hangover, no withdrawal symptoms. But that didn't make it any less scary.

'In the wrong hands it could be a killer,' Jenny said.

47

'Just as well it's in the right hands,' Jed said, at which point there was a ring at the door bell and Jed let in Tubby Moran. He was carrying a crate of bottles, each of them full of a pink liquid, though of a subtly different shade from the stuff Jenny had taken.

'I was up all night,' Tubby said, 'ironing out faults. This stuff is much better.'

'Great,' said Jed, and he took the bottles and loaded them into his fridge. Even given Jed's prodigious rate of drug consumption this huge dosage seemed in excess of requirements.

'My band's doing a gig next Thursday,' he said confidentially. 'Everyone in the audience is going to be given a taste of this stuff as we go on stage. I've got the feeling it could be a very good gig.'

Tubby billowed with pride again, the co-conspirator, the acid prince. Jenny was about to protest that they couldn't do that, but she knew very well that they could and would.

Jenny was in the audience that Thursday to see the Jed Rhodes Band. She took her own supply of drinking water and refused to touch anything anybody offered her. She wanted to be there for this big occasion, but she didn't want to participate in it. She felt someone ought to stay straight, to bear witness, to be ready to call the emergency services if and when necessary.

It occurred to her that if Tubby Moran was wrong, if he hadn't ironed out the problems and everyone in the audience reacted the way she had at the club, then Jed and his band would be forced to play the same song, presumably the opening song of the set, over and over again until the drug wore off. Jed assured her this couldn't happen and she hoped he was right. This new stuff was very cool, very mellow, he said.

As Jed and his band – bass, drums, keyboard player and lead guitarist – took to the stage, the bottles of pink liquid were passed from hand to hand throughout the audience. Some drank more eagerly than others but nobody seemed to be turning it down. Jenny continued to be amazed at the gullible nature of rock audiences.

The band started to play and the audience were appreciative enough. They paid attention, they listened, they cheered enthusiastically at the end of the first couple of songs, but it was all well within the bounds of normal audience response. Then, in the third number, the lead guitarist took a solo. Jenny didn't know his work, didn't even know his name. He was young and muscular and not bad-looking but it seemed to her that the solo was fairly run of the mill. The audience, however, thought differently. From the moment he played the first note of his solo they were bewitched. They hung on his every note, as if they were hearing the music of the spheres. They were truly exultant, truly blissed out. The solo ended and the audience settled down, became sane again, but they had obviously experienced something intense and exquisite and they wanted more.

And that was how it went for the rest of the gig, a perfectly attentive audience that became electrified every time the guitarist took a solo. Jenny watched and wasn't sure what she thought. Should she disapprove? Was something deeply immoral going on here? The artistic objections were obvious enough, but it seemed mean-spirited to object when everyone in the place was having such a spectacularly good time. Jed Rhodes appeared to be having the best time of all. No doubt he'd taken twice as much of the drug as anyone in the audience and the look on his face was positively beatific.

As midnight came around the band tried to take a break, but the audience wouldn't let them leave the stage. They played for another twenty minutes or so, then tried again. This time the audience threatened to turn ugly and demanded encores, dozens of them. The band was forced to play all through the night, to perform every song they knew, and the lead guitarist was forced to play solos until his hands almost bled. Only when the night sky began to lighten with the onset of dawn did the effects of the drug start to wear off. Only then did the audience quieten down and only then were the band allowed to finish.

Jenny left long before the end but she'd already seen more than enough. She didn't get to speak to Jed that night and when she phoned him the next day she was told that he and his band had already left town and started a hastily arranged national tour. She feared the very worst.

Over the next few weeks she heard plenty of rumours, some were more reliable than others and a few were very strange indeed, but they all confirmed that Jed Rhodes was having one helluva tour. All over the country audiences were going crazy for Jed Rhodes, his band, his music, and particularly for his hot young lead guitarist. Jenny read reviews of the gigs, and sometimes the reviewers were mystified by Jed's success with his audience, and she supposed these were reviewers who didn't get to have any of the drug.

But just as often the reviews showed every sign of participation in the drug experience, and were suitably agog in their appreciation. Tickets were selling fast.

The national tour became international. Jed and his band hit the road for America, Japan, the Pacific Rim. Jenny lost touch completely, lost track of his progress, but she did hear that a fifth member of the band had started to appear on stage, an enigmatic little character called Tubby Moran who didn't appear to do much, didn't play a musical instrument, and yet presided over the band as though he were their mascot and guiding genius.

Jenny wished Jed all the best, hoped he'd become rich and famous and able to buy all the drugs he wanted, and on those occasions when she was playing to dull, unresponsive audiences in cold empty halls she wished she could hand round a few draughts of the famous pink liquid. But on balance she never seriously envied Jed. She had a firm sense of impending disaster.

Six months later Jenny was buying some groceries in an all-night supermarket when she saw someone over by the pharmacy counter who looked a lot like Jed Rhodes. She thought it couldn't be him because surely he was still on tour and also because Jed wouldn't look so poor and hollowed out, wouldn't be wearing that shabby old greatcoat, for instance. But she peered down into his shopping trolley, saw that it was full of vodka and cough medicine and she knew it had to be Jed. The face was older, the hair had turned a few shades greyer, the skin too, but it was him all right.

51

'How's it going, Jed?' she asked.

Without lifting his head he said, 'Don't ask, Jenny,' but she couldn't stop herself asking, and later in an all-night coffee bar Jed couldn't help himself telling her the whole sad story.

'Right from the beginning there were problems,' he admitted, 'and I don't deny they were largely caused by drugs. But you know, I've been on other tours where there were problems with drugs, and usually they were drugs a whole lot nastier than Bliss. I thought I could cope. I was stupid, right?'

Jenny didn't reply, so he continued, 'The major problem was getting all the Bliss that we needed. Tubby Moran was a great guy but he was a cottage industry and we needed industrial amounts of the stuff – we were playing to huge audiences remember.

'If he'd stayed home in England and employed a few helpers it might have worked, but he insisted on coming with us and making the stuff while we were on tour. We had to use local ingredients, had to mix up the stuff in the dressing room during sound checks. There were quality control problems. It wasn't that the drug didn't work, just that it could be a little unpredictable.'

'You don't say,' Jenny sniped.

'One night I started the gig with an unaccompanied bass solo and the audience loved it. In fact they loved it so much I had keep on playing it for four hours. They wouldn't let the rest of the band get on stage. Sometimes they loved us so much they wanted to take us home with them and adopt us. Sometimes they loved us so much they wanted to tear us limb from limb. It was weird.

'You probably heard about Tubby demanding to appear on stage with us, and in one way I thought he had a point, because obviously he was vital to the act; it was just that he looked like such a prat on stage. I mean he was completely unmusical. He couldn't dance, couldn't even play a tambourine. He made us look stupid.

'But he was a pussycat compared to my lead guitarist. I know you've got to have plenty of ego in this business and I know that being cheered ecstatically by thousands of people every night must do strange things to your head, but he was ridiculous. He really thought he was the best guitarist who'd ever lived. He really did think he was God and Eric Clapton all rolled into one. He never twigged that it had anything to do with the drug. The worst part of it was that if I happened to be on Bliss at the time I'd think he was right. When the drug wore off, I tried telling him that audiences would have reacted the same way if he'd been a well-trained monkey up there, but he just didn't get it.

'And the rest of the band weren't much better. They got to the stage where they'd only play if the audience was drugged up. They were scared of playing to a straight audience, to anyone who might have their critical faculties intact. They forced me to cancel gigs when Tubby hadn't managed to mix up enough Bliss to get the whole audience loaded.'

Jed shook his head at the terrible memory.

'Still,' said Jenny, 'it can't have been all bad, playing to such adoring audiences.'

'Yeah, on balance I was happy enough but the record company weren't.'

'No?'

'No, because none of the buggers who came to the gigs ever bought any recordings. Maybe they knew it was only a live experience, or maybe one or two had actually bought our records, listened to them and realized they were no good without the drug. I suggested we give away free samples of Bliss with every album, but the record company didn't like that at all.

'So an A&R man took Tubby aside and said to him, couldn't he redesign this drug of his a little so that the effect lasted, either permanently or at least until the punters had bought the CD, taken it home and played it a few times. And couldn't he maybe change the drug so that instead of reacting to raucous guitar noise, the audiences would react instead to strings or middle-of-the-road vocal harmonies. Tubby said he'd see what he could do, but then, of course, the penny dropped. The record company bosses realized they could do without me and the rest of the band. All they needed was Tubby and his drugs. If they could get the right drug to the audience they could put out any old crap and people would still love it and buy it.

'So Tubby Moran, the quisling, got a ten-year "production" deal, and I understand he's going to be working with some very exciting Vegas lounge acts. My lead guitarist decided to go solo and now he plays every night to completely indifferent audiences and wonders where he went wrong. And I'm left with a rhythm section that has lost its nerve. That's how it's going for me. How's it going for you, Jenny?'

Jenny smiled sadly. It seemed she had no worries at all compared to Jed, but the things he'd said had started her thinking. The whole saga of Jed and Tubby and this drug called Bliss had scarcely lasted six months and yet it seemed to her that the drug, or at least something very much like it, had perhaps been around much, much longer than that. If the drug, or a precursor of the drug, had been around for a long time, then who was to say that she, along with millions of others, hadn't already been unknowingly exposed to it.

Its existence explained so much – those albums that only had one listenable track on them, those albums you listened to once and never again, those albums you used to love and nearly wore out with playing that were now completely intolerable, those guitar solos that had once seemed so exciting and vital that now sounded so feeble and pallid.

It explained other things too. Jenny had never been able to understand how anybody could listen to Pat Metheny or John Scofield albums, but mind-altering drugs would certainly have been one way of doing it.

Then another thought struck her. That night in Phoenix when she saw Neil Young, that Free Kitten gig at the Garage in London, watching K. K. Null in Tokyo, they'd all seemed like wonderful, magnificent occasions, but how could she tell that her response had been genuine and not caused by exposure to doses of Bliss? It was a devastating idea.

The next night Jenny Slade and Jed Rhodes did a duo set at a working man's club in Dagenham. It was not one of the great gigs. The audience was restless and halfway through the set a handful of drunks cut up nasty and started heckling and booing. Jed and Jenny smiled and lapped it up. Booing had never sounded so good.

KURT NEVER SLEEPS

'Hey Kurt, where are you going with that gun in your hand?'
Jenny Slade asks brightly.

Kurt spins round. Kurt, a dishwater-blond in a lumberjack
shirt, mascara'd eyes blinking at the vision. He'd thought he
was alone in the room, alone with a head full of storming
emotions, a suitcase full of pharmaceuticals and a few choice
weapons.

'I ain't going nowhere,' he says.

'Well, that's a blessing,' says Jenny. 'And how the hell are
you?'

Stopping to pose, to let his words carry their full cargo,
Kurt says, 'I've hurt myself and I want to die.'

Jenny chuckles politely. 'That's my Kurt, ever the master
of irony.'

We are in the apartment above the garage of Kurt and
Courtney's Madrona home, up in the eaves in a long thin
room, triangular in section, one wall mostly glass. The place
is a mess. Jenny wonders why he doesn't employ a house
cleaner, spread some of that money around, create a little
trickle down.

The books and the CDs and the video tapes have all been

carelessly cast aside. Who would have thought Kurt was such a big reader? Bukowski and Burroughs and Beckett and Burgess. Burgess? Anthony Burgess? Yep – he's one of Kurt's main men. The dog-ears and the split spines testify to Kurt's attention. But then everything has a well-used look around here: wine stains on the rugs, a cigarette stubbed out on the scratch plate of a vintage Fender Jag. Only the weapons and drugs get treated with any respect.

Kurt's guns include a Taurus revolver, a Baretta semi-automatic, a Colt rifle, a Remington twenty-gauge shotgun. His drugs of choice are heroin and Valium; a narcotic cuddle, oblivion with fluffy edges.

'All this loading up on guns and drugs,' Jenny says. 'Tell me about it, Kurt. Do you think it's clever? Do you think it's funny?'

'Well, it makes *me* laugh.'

He turns his back on her and shambles his way over to a desk by the window. There's a writing pad and a few pens set out. The page is filled by a red scrawl, an earlier draft. Kurt picks up a pen, holds it poised in his left hand, then gradually changes his grip till he's holding it not like a pen but a dagger. He slowly stabs the page a few times, making a row of deliberate, calculated gouges. Then he just sits there, blank as a sheet of listing paper, Mr Catatonia.

Jenny lets a few minutes pass before she says, 'Hey Kurt, here I am, entertain me.'

Kurt doesn't smile so she says, 'What are you trying to write anyway? Another chart-topping hit? Another teenage angst-ridden smasheroo?'

'A suicide note if you must know.'

'Cool,' she says, and then, having mulled the matter over, adds, 'It's funny the way we need rock stars to die on us every now and then, isn't it? Like it wakes us up a little. It purifies the tribe, something like that.

'Of course it probably wouldn't happen if you were English. The English really don't have that martyr tradition, not for rock stars anyway. They have a tendency, not necessarily a very attractive one, to keep on living, unless of course they're John Lennon and they meet someone like Mark Whatsisname.'

'Yeah, well I'm not English, OK?'

'Fine.'

'And I'm going to do it just as soon as I finish this damn letter.'

'We could be here all night,' Jenny says, but not loud enough for him to hear. 'I don't suppose anything I say will make any difference.'

'Dead right.'

'And I suppose there's no point in asking you to think about Courtney and the kid.'

'They'll live through this,' Kurt snarls.

'Probably,' Jenny agrees. 'But you couldn't exactly call it responsible parenting, could you now? It can't be exactly what the therapist ordered.'

Kurt turns back to the page, sorry to have wasted time talking. Jenny decides to be helpful. He stares at the paper till his eyes cross and go out of focus.

'When in doubt you could always use a quotation,' Jenny offers.

'Maybe,' says Kurt, 'but I wouldn't want to quote from some old fart.'

'It's a strange thing about people who like popular music,' Jenny says. 'When they're twenty-one they think the best music in the world is made by twenty-one-year olds. When they're forty they think it's made by forty-year olds – sometimes these are the same people they loved when they were twenty-one, but not always.

'Of course, for people who like classical music it's different. They think the only good music is made by dead people.'

Kurt looks at her with narcotic confusion in his eyes. This stuff is hard for him to follow.

'What I'm saying,' Jenny simplifies, 'is that this is what pop music is *for*, surely, to provide a series of shorthand expressions that convey and describe various generalized, uncomplicated feelings.'

Kurt blinks at her in quiet surprise. Well yeah, what she says sounds true if a little fancy. Maybe she's right. Maybe somebody's already said all those things he wants to say.

'How about "It's All Over Now Baby Blue"?' he says hopefully.

'I don't think so,' Jenny replies. 'Dylan's too easy. And before you say it, "I Can't Get No Satisfaction" is too easy as well. How about, "Come On, Do The Jerk"?'

'No,' Kurt says. 'I was never much of a dancer.'

'Then how about "Waiting For The Man"? But no, I can see that wouldn't work, the man's already been and gone. How about "Boom Boom"?'

'Hey, are you taking me for a fool?'

'Not me, Kurt. Any thoughts on what you want to have done with your ashes?'

'Nah, I won't be around to worry about it, will I?'

'So it would be all right for Buddhist students to turn some of them into figurines, and for Courtney to carry the rest of them around inside a teddy bear.'

'Oh sure, like that's really going to happen,' he says, and Jenny doesn't disabuse him.

Suddenly he shouts. 'I know. I've got it. What I need is something from Neil Young. I mean, he's the godfather of grunge, right?'

'I like it,' Jenny agrees. 'Go for it, Kurt. What's it going to be?'

Kurt picks up the guitar, strums a few easy, unamplified Neil Young chords, then says, 'Yeah, I got it. I got it.'

'Great,' Jenny says enthusiastically, and she watches as Kurt takes up the pen again and writes across the page those immortal words 'I've been a miner for a heart of gold – and I'm gettin' old,' and signs it with a flourish.

'Oh come on, Kurt,' Jenny says irritatedly. 'I know your brains are scrambled but you can do better than that.'

Kurt shivers. The room is suddenly cold and the desk looks as big as a pool table. He doesn't think he can do better than that at all.

She feels sorry for him, and takes his hand and guides it as it writes down a far better Neil Young line, the one about rust and fade. Kurt looks at the words on the page and feels pleased with himself. Jenny seems pleased with him too. She looks out of the window. She can see water, trees, hedges, a well-kept lawn. It's OK here. A young couple and their baby could lead a very comfortable, privileged life in this place if they had a mind to.

'Hey, I think I've got a better line,' she says.

But it's too late. Behind her the shotgun goes off and Kurt turns himself into a sort of hero, a member of the stupid club.

Jenny shrugs, looks at her watch. It's still early. She wishes he'd hung around and at least offered some advice to the aspiring guitarist. She wishes he'd at least waited until she'd told him to use a better Neil Young line. 'Got mashed potato. Ain't got no T-bone.' That's what she'd have recommended. But maybe Kurt wouldn't have liked that so much. He never looked much like a T-bone kind of guy.

PERFORMANCE NOTES

Bob Arnold reviews a Jenny Slade gig and decides she's the Po-Mo queen of the guitar.

The Club Tutto, Milan: a converted small arms factory on a hot September night in the early nineties. Jenny Slade and the latest incarnation of the Flesh Guitars bounce on to the stage, an all-girl, drummerless line-up; girls who look part punkette, part pagan. They wave encouragingly at the audience, then each picks up a guitar from the stands on the edge of the stage. They strap them on. There's the noise of jack plugs being slid into sockets, of volume and tone controls being whirled, the static of pickup selector switches being moved, the sighing of a wah wah pedal being pumped.

The audience, a thousand or so hot-blooded souls, is all antici-pation, and the apparently slow start only adds to its eagerness, its readiness and willingness to be entertained. Still, the band continue to fiddle with their instruments and equipment. Amp settings are adjusted, effects boxes are switched on and off. Sometimes there's hiss, sometimes buzz, sometimes a suggestion of muted feedback, of a sort of ambient reverb; but there is nothing remotely resembling music. No guitar is strummed, no chord is played, certainly nobody attempts anything resembling a guitar solo. The audience experience and show a little restlessness, but still the girls of the Flesh Guitars continue flicking dials and knobs, making endless minute adjustments. And then suddenly the audience *gets it.*

They realize they are listening to the sound, not of music, but of the conditions that make music possible, the sound of electricity, of signal to noise ratios, to the imperfections of circuitry, to interference.

After half an hour or so the whole audience is completely rapt, is in complete awe. Someone says, in unaccented English, loud enough for others to hear, 'Lord have mercy, Jenny Slade and the Flesh Guitars are forcing us to wholly redefine our conceptions both of music and of performance.'

The show continues for three hours or so in much the same way, gathering majesty and grandeur as it progresses, or rather fails to progress, after which the Flesh Guitars receive a fifteen-minute standing ovation and, despite much pleading, decline to come back for an encore.

The performance, untitled at the time, is now universally known as *Totally Tutto.* It exists in at least three recorded versions. All have merit, but connoisseurs find the Milanese rendering far and away the best.

Reprinted from the *Journal of Sladean Studies*
Volume 6 Issue 9

A GIG LIKE ALICE

Jenny Slade was in Alice Springs, Australia, a guest of the well-respected and only moderately under-funded Red Centre Improvised Music Festival. She had spent the last week playing in unlikely duos, trios and sometimes larger ensembles, along with Aboriginal percussionists, dancers, flute and didgeridoo players, as well as with various imported international free jazzers, avant-garde rockers and classical musicians who were prepared to let themselves go and take a few risks. It had all been cool but exhausting, and now that it was over she was sitting in the festival bar talking to Billy Nation, an Aboriginal cello player who'd had some success writing music for theatre and television, though he made it plain that his real ambition was to create music much more profound, much more spiritual than that.

'So let me get this straight,' Jenny said. 'The Aboriginal myths tell of legendary ancestors who, in Dreamtime, wandered all over the continent singing out the name of everything they came across; not only naming birds and animals and plants the way Adam supposedly did, but also naming hills, rivers, valleys, mountain ranges.'

'That's right,' Billy said draining a tube of lager. 'And in that way the ancestors sang the world into being.'

'But I'm not sure I quite understand that,' Jenny said. 'By definition if they were giving names to things, the things must already have existed.'

'None of this is easy for the white, western mind to understand,' Billy said. 'You see, each ancestor is thought to have left a trail of music and words along the route he travelled. So a song becomes a map and a direction finder. If you know the song, you know your way across the whole country.'

Jenny wasn't quite sure he was answering the question she'd asked, but she let him go on.

'The man who goes walkabout,' Billy Nation continued, 'is making a sacred journey, reliving his ancestor's journey and singing his song as he goes.'

'And the subjects of all these songs are holy?' Jenny asked.

'That's right; every rock, every waterhole, every cliff face, they're all sacred sites, because our ancestors sang about them in Dreamtime.'

'I guess that pushes up real estate values too.'

Billy frowned at her and she looked apologetic. She knew it was a cheap shot.

'I've never been much of a singer myself,' Jenny admitted. 'I have enough trouble staying in tune without having to sing a continent into being.'

Billy smiled indulgently. He was prepared to be charitable, if lordly, towards this white woman and her jokes.

'You aren't going to be able to understand any of this from the festival bar,' he said. 'You have to experience the songlines, see them *in situ*. If you had a couple of days, I could take you up country so you could meet some real local musicians, people for whom music and breathing are one and the same thing. You could play for them and they could play for you.'

Jenny took the offer at its face value and said OK. She could tell that Billy was surprised and not necessarily pleased. He obviously never imagined that she'd take him up on it, and perhaps he hadn't thought through all the implications of travelling into the bush with a strange white woman, but now that she'd accepted, he was too proud to withdraw or modify his offer. The trip was on.

Billy Nation turned up next day at Jenny Slade's hotel in a battered old Land Cruiser, decked out with roo bars, sand ladders, spare petrol cans and tyres. It was thickly powdered with oxidized red sand, as if it were trying to camouflage itself and blend in with the earth.

Billy's cello took up very little space inside the Land Cruiser. Jenny loaded up her own gear, and Billy drove away from the civilization of Alice Springs into the low, blank desert landscape. As they drove along increasingly unmade roads the equipment in the back rattled and bounced around as though creating some long, free-form percussion solo. Jenny feared breakages but Billy was oblivious. She wondered whether he would put a cassette into the stereo, wondered what music he'd think appropriate for the trip, but the player remained unused, Billy preferring to hear the song of the wind and the road.

Jenny Slade stared at the slowly undulating land, at the anonymous dirt road, the endless low scrub and said, 'It looks like an easy place to get lost in.'

Billy Nation smiled the smile of a man with inner knowledge and wisdom, and didn't deign to reply.

'So who are these people we're going to see?' Jenny asked.

'Good guys. The best.'

'What do they play?'

Billy seemed to be thinking long and hard about his reply. 'I guess you'd have to call it country music,' he said. He laughed and Jenny laughed with him. She was beginning to understand. If the country itself was created by song, then how could there be anything other than country music?

They drove on and on into the red vastness, wrecked cars by the roadside, kangaroos and emus bouncing in the middle distance, disused mines and shacks on the horizon. Jenny lost track of the time but when Billy eventually stopped the Land Cruiser after three hours or so, she was glad of the break. They appeared to be absolutely nowhere, a scrubby bit of outback no different from the last hundred miles of terrain they'd passed through, but Billy, she assumed, saw it differently.

He got out of the Land Cruiser and headed for the nearest high place, a mound of red sand that was not really very high at all, but he climbed it, stood on top and scanned the territory, exalting, as if reclaiming it for himself. She let him stand alone there for a long time before she went to join him.

'It's a big, big place,' she said.

'Even bigger when you're lost,' Billy added.

She looked at him and smiled to acknowledge his dry wit, but he didn't smile back. He wasn't being witty.

'Yeah, OK, all right,' he said defensively. 'I'm lost, OK, I'm lost.'

'What, do you mean you don't know the songlines for this area?'

'That's one way of stating the problem,' he said, sounding peevish and urban now, not at all the attuned man of the desert she'd set out with.

'Don't you have a map in the truck?' she asked.

'If I had a map I wouldn't be lost.'

He slunk away, brooding and simmering in silence. Jenny looked around. The lack of landmarks was startling. There was nothing at all to navigate by. She caught up with Billy.

'Well,' she said positively, 'not so very long ago we passed a mining camp. We could drive back and ask them for directions.'

'It was at least fifty miles back,' Billy said bleakly. 'I don't have enough petrol to get us there.'

'Oh dear,' said Jenny.

'I had other things on my mind, all right?' Billy said, defending himself from accusations Jenny had no need to voice.

'We could light a fire,' Jenny suggested. 'A distress signal.'

'No matches,' Billy said, and before she could suggest anything else he added, 'It gets worse. I don't have any food and I only brought half a pint of water.'

She looked at him as though he were a subhuman idiot.

'Is it my fault if I was brought up in a suburb of Melbourne?' he whined. 'I just read about the songlines in a book, like everyone else.'

It was late afternoon. At least the sun was past its hottest point. They stood in silence not daring to look at each other, having absolutely nothing to say. Jenny thought of the various forms of murderous revenge she could take on him and feared that the land might do the job for her all too soon.

'There is one possibility,' he said weakly at last. 'As it happens I always carry a portable generator with me, just in case. It's petrol driven. I could siphon the last of the petrol out of the Land Cruiser and then we'd have a little power.'

'And then?'

'And then you could play your guitar.'

'I'm not in the mood for a jam session.'

'I'd do it myself but a cello isn't the same.'

'What are you on about?'

'You'd play the guitar very, very loud. The noise would carry for miles. Somebody would hear it and come and see what it was all about. They'd have food and water, maybe even petrol. At the very least they could tell us where we were.'

It sounded like an idiotic plan to Jenny but she couldn't think of anything better so she agreed to it. They unloaded the necessary equipment from the Land Cruiser and set it up at the roadside. Billy siphoned the petrol, brought the generator to life and Jenny was ready to play. It was hard to know what was the right repertoire for such a venue and such a gig, but she started to improvise a long, searing, high-pitched solo and she hoped that somebody, somewhere could hear it.

It was getting dark now and as her notes spread out over the emptiness, the enterprise seemed increasingly absurd. She felt they were wasting precious energy that they might need later for survival. The darkness gathered, night thickened, and the sound of Jenny's guitar became ever more lonesome, ever more forlorn. It seemed an utterly futile activity.

Suddenly, as she was thinking of giving up, out of the darkness a boy appeared. He was a young, shaggy-haired Aboriginal, perhaps twelve years old, in shorts and bare feet. The moment Jenny saw him she stopped playing and they stood looking at each other in wary silence. She was going to speak when the boy turned his back and began to walk away. She called after him but he didn't stop or reply so she struck a loud power chord and he turned and beckoned for her to follow him. She unhooked her guitar and was about to put it down, but he gestured again and indicated that he wanted her to bring the guitar with him. He further indicated that Billy Nation should bring the amplifier. Billy protested for a moment but the boy was having none of it. If they wanted his help he'd have to bring the amp. Above all else Billy did not want to be left alone in the outback, so he picked up the big amp and speaker cabinet and the three of them proceeded through the bush in a curious little procession.

They hadn't travelled far before they came to a large tin shed built on the bank of a dried-out river bed. There was a row of lights along the edge of the roof and the sound of a jukebox coming from within. The boy held open the split wooden door and Jenny went inside, closely followed by Billy Nation in his new role as roadie.

There were perhaps thirty people inside the hut, mostly young and mostly Aboriginal, though not exclusively either.

A bar made out of beer crates ran along one side of the room, and the walls were painted an insistent canary yellow. There was a drum kit set up in one corner, along with a microphone and a beautiful, battered old piano with sconces and fretwork.

The crowd looked at Jenny with curiosity, but with a strange lack of surprise, as though guest guitarists were always dropping in. There was no doubt that she was expected to play, that she was expected to impress, and the matter of where they were or where they might obtain petrol, food and water would have to wait.

Fuming, Billy Nation set down the amp and Jenny plugged in. She continued to play in the same style as she had been in the desert. She was trying to pick up on the spirit of the place, on the stark emptiness, and it seemed to require something both beautiful and desolate. However, after playing for five minutes or so she could see that the audience in the hut was losing interest. She carried on, trying that much harder, but they just weren't keen on what she was doing. Jenny stopped playing, hoping for inspiration. She turned towards Billy Nation but his face was blank and inscrutable. He was as much a stranger here as she was. He was going to be no help at all. Then the boy who'd brought them edged towards Jenny, put his mouth close to her ear and said, 'Generally what goes down best is some pretty basic rock and roll.'

Jenny could take a hint. She immediately changed tack and started to play a variety of rock and roll favourites: 'Johnny B. Goode', 'Lucille', 'Something Else'. 'Route 66' went down particularly well. A young guy got up and sat in on drums, another sat at the piano and did a pretty good impression of Little Richard. Jenny played gorgeous chunky rock and roll solos, and at one point was moved to perform a duck walk. The crowd loved her for it. The place was so alive, so enthusiastic she feared it might spontaneously combust. The only damper was Billy Nation who sat nursing a beer, his face showing absolute sulky disapproval.

After an hour or so of fierce rock and roll, the boy came up to her again and pointed out an old man leaning on the bar, a man with a face as ancient as the rocks and the sand. The boy whispered, 'The old fellah says can you play anything by Jimmy Webb?'

And so they played a short medley of Jim Webb hits, including 'By The Time I Get To Phoenix', before returning to rock and roll. There was the same frenzy and adulation, and then all too suddenly it was over and the bar was emptying and Jenny was sipping a drink, feeling doubly exhausted and triply satisfied. Someone gave her a crate of beer and someone else provided a map and pointed out that they were only a couple of miles from a roadhouse and Shell station.

Jenny accepted as graciously, as gratefully, as she knew how, all too aware of the sullen, graceless presence of Billy Nation. She no longer felt any need to chastise or berate him, but neither did she feel any responsibility.

She said to him, 'You know, I've been thinking about the way certain American popular songs can be used as songlines. Look at "By The Time I Get To Phoenix". When she's rising he's in Phoenix, then when she's having her lunch he's in Albuquerque, and by the time she gets home from work he's made Oklahoma. You could draw his journey on a map.

'Or how about "Route 66"? Some of it's just a list of names: Missouri, St Louis, Oklahoma City and so on. Follow the names and you could never get lost. Isn't that exactly what a songline is?'

Billy shook his head at her sadly and with all the condescension he could muster. He was trying to imply that she was stupid, that all she had done was confirm that she was too crass ever to understand him or his culture, and perhaps ultimately that was true, but there was some consolation in knowing she had the ability to play to an audience, any audience, and entertain them and make them happy.

Billy Nation walked out into the night and Jenny was about to shout something mildly abusive after him, to tell him to get lost, but she decided that was no longer necessary.

BEAUTY TIPS WITH JENNY SLADE:

Number one: the nails

Jenny Slade says, 'You know a lot of women seem to think that in order to get that authentic snarly, slutty, rock chick look, they have to wear their fingernails as long and sharp as talons, and that they should be painted blood red or Goth black, or in some metallic cyber shade. But I'm afraid it's not that simple.

'There are two problems here. One, a right-handed guitarist can't have talons on her left hand at all, because if she does they'll get in the way of holding down the strings.

'Secondly, even the strongest non-chip enamel will get trashed by the time you've played two hours worth of shred and burn guitar, especially if you do any amount of finger picking. And, despite Courtney Love, most of us still believe that chipped nail varnish is a sin second only to a visible panty line. You could use false nails, I suppose, but in my humble opinion false nails are an abomination against nature.

'So you see, my advice to young female guitar players is really pretty simple: keep the natural look at your fingertips. Get a good manicure, eat gelatine, keep your nails short and unpainted. Let the authentic snarly, slutty, rock chick persona come from your playing, not just from your cosmetics.'

Reprinted from the *Journal of Sladean Studies*
Volume 3 Issue 12

CONDUCT UNBECOMING

Jenny Slade was staying in a tourist hotel in Haiti when she first met Tom Scorn. She was lying out by the pool, eyes closed, gently working on her tan, slowly working off a queen-size hangover, when she became aware of someone casting a shadow over her face. She opened her eyes, looked up and saw a scrawny, thick-lipped young guy standing there, apparently trying to summon the courage to speak. He was tall, had spiked hair and big eyes, and now that she was actually looking at him, his first reaction was to run away, but he steeled himself, swallowed and said, perhaps a little too loudly, as though he had been rehearsing it, 'Miss Slade, I'd like to say how much I've always enjoyed your music.'

Jenny was not entirely unused to receiving such compliments, nor to dealing with them efficiently, and she handled it as gracefully as she could. 'You're very kind,' she said. 'Thank you.'

Sometimes this exchange would be enough, but more usually it would be followed by a request for an autograph, which she usually agreed to, or by an attempt to involve her in a muso conversation about guitars and guitarists, which she was skilled at avoiding. But this particular boy did none of the usual things. He wouldn't go away but neither would he say anything more.

When the situation had become unbearable Jenny said, 'Is there something else I can do for you?'

'Well maybe,' he said. 'I'm a music student.'

Jenny was unimpressed.

'Actually I'm studying piano, saxophone and composition, with particular reference to Stockhausen, Cardew, Wally Stott. And yourself.'

'That's very nice,' Jenny said, though she wasn't really sure it was nice at all.

She saw that he was carrying a tan leather music case and he now held it up in front of him like a breastplate.

'I have some of my compositions in here,' he said, sounding simultaneously proud and diffident. 'Maybe you'd like to take a look at one or two of them.'

Jenny had a firm rule about not accepting things that strangers shoved into her hands. If she was handed a demo tape she knew it would be dreadful and incompetent and unlistenable, but nevertheless the makers of the tape were all too likely to sue her for plagiarism at a later date. If she was handed a note, a piece of 'creative writing' perhaps, it would inevitably be somebody's sick little sex fantasy. If somebody gave her drugs they would always be tainted. So she made it a rule not to accept gifts from strangers and she was on the point of saying a firm no, when the boy began to fiddle with the case and it fell open so that sheets of manuscript paper spilled out and scurried across the poolside tiles towards the water. Jenny put out a hand and lazily caught one sheet while the boy headed off to catch the more fugitive pages.

She intended to hand the page straight back without looking at it, but she couldn't help noticing that the paper in her hand was a cover sheet, a title page that read 'Forty Guitar Solos for Jenny Slade' by Tom Scorn'. She liked guitar solos and couldn't help being intrigued.

'You're Tom Scorn?' she said.

'Yes. It's my composition.'

'Show me the rest of it,' she said.

He dipped into the case and fiddled again. She hoped the music wasn't too complex. Like all the best guitarists her sight-reading was pretty rudimentary.

'Here you are,' he said, handing over a bundle of paper, some of it creased, some of it damp around the edges.

She saw that she needn't have worried. The pages contained words rather than musical notes, quite a lot of words she noticed, rather too many to absorb all at once.

'OK if I take this away with me?' she asked.

Tom Scorn sighed as though all his dreams had come true.

'What if you need to get in touch with me?' he asked.

'I'll find a way,' she said, and she waved him away, not with contempt but with finality, and once he was out of sight she began to read his compositions.

FORTY GUITAR SOLOS FOR JENNY SLADE, COMPOSED BY TOM SCORN

(In these compositions it is assumed that the guitarist is right handed and plays a conventionally strung instrument. Left-handers should make the appropriate reversals.)

1) The Lubrication Solo
The player takes a guitar and places it on a stand so that it is upright, leaning backwards at a slight angle. She opens a two-gallon tin of motor oil and pours its contents down the neck of the guitar, varying the rate and quantity of oil so as to vary the sound produced. She continues until the tin is empty.

2) The Spherical Solo
The player arranges a number of different guitars on stage. She then moves to the back of the hall where there is a large pile of balls of various sizes and weights and densities. The player hurls these balls one at a time at the guitars on stage, attempting to hit them cleanly on the strings, but inevitably inaccuracies will occur. Some balls will miss the strings, hit the guitar's body or machine heads, with rich unpredictable results.

(Possible projectiles include cricket balls, baseballs, cotton-wool balls, footballs, meat balls and, at outdoor winter gigs, snowballs.)

3) The Hot Solo
With her left hand the player begins to play the chord changes of a standard I–IV–V progression ('Louie Louie', 'Wild Thing', *et al*). In her other hand she now takes an ignited blow lamp

and 'strums' the strings with the flame until either the strings melt or the guitar body catches fire. (The noise subsequently created by the use of the fire extinguisher is to be considered part of the solo.)

4) The Fall Solo

The player selects a number of guitars, tunes them to Open E and places them under the spreading branches of a large deciduous tree on a breezy day in mid-autumn. As the leaves fall they land on the strings and play fragile, delicate notes and half chords.

5) The Blackboard Solo

The player holds down a chord of C 7th. She then inserts three sticks of chalk (which may be coloured or plain white) between the fingers of the right hand and rubs them hard up and down the guitar neck so that they crumble and snap and disintegrate. The solo continues until the chalk is completely pulverized and there's nothing in the hand but chalk dust.

6) The Spanking Solo

The player inserts a thin plank of wood between the guitar strings and the fingerboard. Using a hand saw she then starts to cut the plank. The solo consists of the vibrations and movement passed through the plank to the strings and the guitar. It ends when the plank is sawn through.

7) The Inflated Solo

The player holds a guitar horizontally. She takes six balloons and fills them with helium and varying amounts of gravel. One balloon is attached to each guitar string, so that the balloons float at various points above the guitar. Slowly, and with feeling, the player bursts each balloon in turn so that gravel showers down on the strings and body of the guitar.

8) The Stubble Solo

The player coats the guitar strings in lime-scented shaving foam. She then takes a disposable razor, preferably one with a swivel action head, and proceeds to give the strings a very close shave.

(Depilatory cream might be used as an acceptable alternative, but the use of hot wax would constitute a different composition, as would the use of an electric razor.)

9) The Dog Solo

The player finds a large dog, preferably of a bouncy, good-natured variety, and uses a length of string to attach the dog's tail to the whammy bar of her guitar. The player now attempts to perform a version of the Shadows' 'Apache', while the dog expresses its natural exuberance. The piece ends when dog and player can stand it no longer.

10) The Literate Solo

The player takes a text, preferably an English classic, and places it on a music stand in front of her. She begins to read the text silently to herself. Each time the word 'the' appears in the text the player strums the chord of B minor. Each time the word 'a' appears she strums the chord of A minor 7th. Each time the word 'and' occurs she strums the chord of C 6th. The piece may be of any length.

11) The Explosive Solo

The player takes three or four fireworks, say a Snowstorm, a Mount Stromboli, a Roman Candle and an Air Bomb Repeater,

and weaves them in and out of the strings of her guitar. She
then lights the blue touch paper and listens very carefully.

12) The Stretched Solo

The player stands on stage firmly holding a guitar. (A guitar
strap should not be employed.) Two powerful bungee cords
are used to attach the guitar to the back wall of the hall. The
player strums diminished chords until, as the spirit takes her,
she lets go of her guitar and watches it fly through the air and
strike the back wall to produce remarkable sonic effects.

13) The Cool Solo

The player begins to perform a series of blues-based hammer-
ons and pull-offs and slides with the fingers of her left hand.
She then takes an aerosol of freezing medical spray and directs
it at the playing hand, continuing until that hand loses all
feeling and playing becomes impossible.

14) The Tinsnip Solo

The player sets up her guitar to produce a low, regular, howling
feedback. She then takes a pair of tinsnips and cuts each string
in turn, from low to high E.

15) The Restrained Solo

The left and right wrists of the player are put into two separate
pairs of handcuffs by an assistant. The free handcuff on the
left wrist is closed around the neck of the guitar, the free
handcuff on the right wrist is closed around the strings close to
the bridge. Thus restricted and with the loops of the handcuffs
rattling against the strings, the player now attempts a rendition
of 'I Fought The Law'.

16) The Errol Flynn Solo

(It is said that, as a party piece, Errol Flynn used to take out his penis and let it drop on the piano keyboard to play individual notes and form a tune. How much more impressive if he'd played the guitar.)

The player attaches a rubber dildo to herself (she may be naked or fully clothed as she pleases) and holds the guitar in such a way that she can use the dildo to strum the chords of 'Mull Of Kintyre'.

17) The Sub-Errol Flynn Solo

The player holds a guitar in front of her in a phallic posture. She bangs the neck of the guitar against a microphone stand until one or other droops.

18) The Free-Range Solo

The player takes half a dozen hen's eggs and smashes them at various places on her guitar. She then takes an egg whisk and beats the eggs, and to an extent the guitar as well, until small peaks appear.

19) The Considerate Solo

The player holds a guitar in one hand and a house brick in the other. She considers the myriad possibilities, but does nothing.

20) The Prophylactic Solo

A large, opaque plastic bag is placed over the guitar and the player must wrest sounds from the instrument through the plastic.

(In a minor variation of this solo the plastic bag may be placed over the player instead.)

21) The Tarmac Solo

The player uses a two-hundred-yard-long lead to connect the guitar to the amplifier. She then picks up the guitar, leaves the stage, leaves the auditorium, and goes out into the nearest road, which should be only intermittently busy with traffic. The player sets the guitar down in the centre of the road and returns to the hall. The solo is 'played' when the first vehicle runs over the guitar, an incident which is not seen and is heard only as electrical noise conveyed along the lead. The player may be in or out of the hall when this happens.

(If the player only owns one guitar it is recommended that this piece be played as the last solo of the evening.)

There were another nineteen or so 'compositions' in a similar vein. When she had read them all Jenny Slade put down the pages, smiled and said, 'I'll gig.' She tracked down Tom Scorn and agreed to play a series of solo concerts in which she would showcase these creations of his. She thought of it as a way of giving a helping hand to a young, up and coming musician.

Somewhat to her surprise he said he had already taken the first steps towards booking such a tour and had used her name to obtain an Arts Council grant. The guy was obviously quite a hustler. He was also decidedly well organized and well connected. He booked her into a variety of cabaret clubs, avant-garde jazz venues and small concert halls. He insisted on travelling with her and attending every date on the tour, saying he might need to rewrite or modify the compositions as they went along. She thought this was a mite over-conscientious and it certainly upped the travelling expenses, but she didn't complain.

Neither did she complain when she saw that the posters for the early concerts read, 'Jenny Slade plays the music of Tom Scorn'. As the senior partner she thought that her name ought to be bigger than his, rather than equal size, although at least hers came first. But as the tour progressed (and it was not a very long tour) the poster was redesigned so that it read, 'Tom Scorn guitar solos, played by Jenny Slade'. This was, she supposed, factually accurate but she still believed that she was the draw, rather than this young, unknown composer. When the tour hit Amsterdam, Scorn decided that 'guitar solos' was not a sufficiently beguiling title so he came up with another, and now the posters read, 'Thomas Scorn's First Guitar Symphony', and then in much smaller print, 'Soloist, Jenny Slade'.

At this point Jenny did complain, loudly and at length, but Scorn seemed so young and enthusiastic, so naive, that it was hard to be very angry with him. And besides, she did enjoy playing the music; it was challenging and different, and audiences liked it. You could forgive a lot as long as things were going well on stage.

But things came to a complete head in a club in Wiesbaden when, two minutes before Jenny was due to go on stage, Scorn announced that he intended to conduct her performance. He'd bought a baton and a tailcoat specially for the occasion. It was too late to have a full blown argument about it and, short of kicking him off stage, Jenny didn't know what she could do. She played her way through the solos, ignoring him as much as she could, refusing to make eye contact, and trying her best to make it clear to the audience that she was not being in any way conducted.

As the final chords of the last solo trickled away, Tom Scorn stood directly in front of her and bowed grandly to the audience. It was as if she did not exist for him any more, as if he alone had created the music out of nothing. He lapped up the applause and didn't even offer a gesture of acknowledgement towards Jenny.

When she could stand it no longer she kicked him hard in the backside, so hard that he *had* to acknowledge her presence. He spun round, and she spun round too and she was holding her guitar at head height so that it swung like a tennis racket or indeed a frying pan, and Tom Scorn's face made hard, sickening contact with the guitar, just a little way above the bridge, so that the strings started to vibrate and set up a long, aching discord.

'That was a composition of my own,' Jenny said. '"The Dickhead Composer Solo."'

When his face had stopped pulsating Tom Scorn said coolly, ever needing to take credit, 'No, Jenny, that was a *duet*.'

QUARTER TO THREE . . .

'All right,' says Kate, 'you've given me the historical background, but I think there's a paradox in all this, don't you? Wouldn't you say that we're discussing the intellectual background to what is an anti-intellectual form?'

'I don't think rock music is anti-intellectual,' Bob says passionately. 'And as a matter of fact neither does Jenny Slade. Neither she nor I have ever really believed in the guitar player as noble savage. We believe in instinct, of course, but it's surprising how much better a player's instincts can get when he's got a brain that's in working order. It seems to me that those years Jenny Slade spent at the Sorbonne, at Oxford, at Harvard, they all went into making her the shit-hot guitarist she is today.'

Kate says, 'You make Jenny Slade sound like a blue stocking.'

'A blue stocking maybe,' Bob admits, 'but blue stockings worn with high heels and a suspender belt.'

Kate is amused. The kid has a way with words. He also has a way with Scotch. His glass is already empty again and she fills it up. He looked like such a shy, sober lad when he came in.

'OK, so you've explained the significance of the electric guitar,' she says. 'Now explain the significance of Jenny Slade.'

Bob takes a deep breath. He's been waiting for this and he's more than ready.

'Right,' he says. 'So the electric guitar has been around for, say, sixty years. The modern idea of pop music, by which I suppose I mean rock and roll, has been around for maybe a couple of decades less. In that time various women performers have been strident, brilliant, self-destructive, tragic, outrageous, unreasonable, suicidal. They've been all the things that men have been, good and bad, and yet the idea of a great female guitarist, the guitar heroine, remains an untried concept.

· 'Now you may say look at Jennifer Batten or Lita Ford, in which case I'd say *get real*. They're just drag acts, bad male impersonators. Or you may say that the electric guitar just isn't a girl thing. You'll say that the *acoustic* guitar is a girl thing (look at Joni Mitchell or Suzanne Vega), you'll say the *bass* guitar is sometimes a girl thing (look at Suzi Quatro, "lewd in leather", look at Tina Weymouth, "tempting with a trust fund"). But skronking female lead guitar, you'll say, it's a rare bird. And all I can say is it's also a damn shame.

'That's where Jenny Slade comes in. She comes down the front of the stage, turns the volume to twelve, puts her foot up on the monitor, gives it some welly, and just *does it*. And she does it right, for real, like nobody else, certainly not like some man.

'I don't know why it should be so unusual for a woman to do that, but it is. The very idea of Jenny Slade, guitar heroine, seems utterly strange, utterly subversive. Sometimes it seems inconceivable, like science fiction or something, but there's Jenny Slade confirming that it's all possible and true.'

'Hold on,' says Kate, 'that wasn't exactly what happened here tonight. She didn't exactly turn up to twelve, put her foot up and give it some welly at all. It was far spookier than that.'

'Precisely,' Bob says with delight and triumph. 'That's why she's special. She's so infinitely surprising, so infinitely various. Whatever expectations you have she confounds them, yet she still delivers. She doesn't just give you what you want, she gives you what you never even knew existed or even thought was possible. But once she's delivered it, you realize it was what you wanted all along.'

Kate nods. What he says makes surprising sense. What he's described is precisely the experience she had earlier that night. He's not only explaining Jenny Slade, he's also explaining Kate's own feelings. He may look like a joke but he knows his stuff.

'Have you ever met her?' she asks.

'Of course. I am her number one fan, after all.'

He digs in his briefcase and produces an autograph album. He opens it, and there on the first page it says, 'To Bob Arnold, my number one fan. Love, Jenny Slade'.

'Well, I guess that proves it,' Kate says, unimpressed.

'No, that doesn't prove it,' he snarls defensively.

'What proves it is that I have here *two hundred* Jenny Slade autographs,' and he flips the pages of the book so that she can see Jenny Slade's autograph on every page.

Kate, naturally, still doesn't think that proves anything

except that Bob is obsessive and weird, so he tries another technique.

'I'll convince you,' he says. 'I have all her recordings, OK? How's that for starters? And I do mean all of them, in all formats and all sort of pressings, all the remixes and all the bonus tracks, all the picture discs and fold-out sleeves, the rare imported box sets, promotional items, Japanese twelve inchers, radio edits. I have acetates and bootlegs and un-released demos.'

'OK,' Kate says, a little impressed, prepared to allow that this is some reasonable definition of fandom.

'But that's only the tip of the iceberg,' Bob laughs. 'There's all the merchandise too. I buy the goods: the T-shirts, the baseball caps, the posters, the concert programmes. I snip cuttings out of magazines and stick them in scrapbooks; dozens of scrapbooks. I hang out at record fairs and swap meets, looking for those unknown, unlisted rarities. I com-municate with other fans, by post, by fax, by Internet, argu-ing with them to prove that my fandom is predominant.

'I've been to hundreds of Jenny Slade gigs, of course. I've travelled tens of thousands of miles to see her. I've got thirty or so plectrums and a dozen or more broken strings that I've picked up off the stage after gigs. I have her used towels and sweat bands, and even a grubby T-shirt she threw into the audience at a concert in Bruges. I had to fight dirty to get that.

'Maybe all that makes me a bit of an anorak, but at least it's an anorak with a picture of Jenny Slade appliquéd on the back.'

'OK, you're her number one fan,' Kate concedes.

'And,' Bob adds passionately, 'as if that wasn't enough I came to this hell-hole trying to see her play, didn't I?'

Kate considers this and is doubly, triply, impressed. She has to admit that coming all this way to the Havoc Bar and Grill, to a place where they'd normally eat people like him alive, for a performance that was neither advertised nor expected does show a formidable degree of commitment, of manic fandom.

'But if you really want to see how great my fandom is,' Bob says determinedly, 'all you have to do is read this.'

He puts a copy of a magazine on the bar. It's a fanzine, not badly produced, well printed, neatly designed, and bearing the title *JOSS*.

'Joss?' Kate asks.

'*Journal of Sladean Studies*. Jenny Slade. Get it?'

'I get it all right.'

'I wanted something with an academic ring to it. I'm the publisher, picture researcher, distributor, proof reader, fact checker and chief scribe. There's something in here you ought to read.'

He opens the magazine, folds it at the appropriate page and turns it round for her to see. She looks at it quizzically. This night is getting more and more bizarre. She's been asked to do some weird things by previous customers of the Havoc Bar and Grill, but reading articles in academic journals is the most bizarre yet. Nevertheless she looks at the piece, which is short; she looks at the time, which is still not all that late, and she decides she has nothing much to lose. She begins to read.

THE RECORD LIBRARY OF BABEL

(A true fan's account)

The universe (which others call the 'Record Library') is composed of an indefinite and perhaps infinite number of hexagonal listening booths. (The term 'Record Library' may seem both archaic and anachronistic, given that vinyl has long since been abandoned and superseded by the compact disc. However the word 'record' remains the most appropriate, since the Library undoubtedly still contains recordings, and since it is also an agency of record.)

The layout of the booths is invariable. There is salmon-pink carpet, a leather couch and state-of-the-art listening equipment. The walls are soundproofed and in two of them, as well as in the floor and ceiling, there is a hatchway that leads into a sort of airlock which interconnects with other hexagonal listening booths, like a honeycomb. Within the booths are toilet facilities, and listeners can sleep comfortably enough on the sofas.

In each listening booth four walls have floor to ceiling storage units consisting of ten shelves. Each shelf then contains sixty single CDs and each CD lasts approximately seventy minutes. There is a letter or number on the spine of each CD case, but there is no packaging, no cover art, no liner notes and no track listings. These letters and numbers bear no apparent relation to the content of each disc, which consists solely and entirely of guitar solos.

Like all men of the Record Library, I have travelled in my youth. I wandered in search of inspiration, in search of a brand new, totally original guitar sound which would say and do it all. I visited listening booths at the far extremities of the system, pushed and exhausted myself. It was a long, hard struggle but worth it, since in the process I discovered the music of Jenny Slade.

Theories have always circulated about the nature, the extent and the 'meaning' of the Record Library. It has been much admired, much praised. People have dedicated far more of their lives to exploring its treasures than I have. The most fanatical have asserted that it is proof of the existence of God since (they argue) such a neat, vast and methodical library could only be created by a supreme being, and one who, incidentally, likes to rock. Man, the imperfect listener, the music enthusiast, the obsessive fan, is compelled to feel awe in the face of such a magnificent creation. He must also be content to realize that he will never fully know or comprehend it.

However, some generations ago, a Ph.D. student and part-time disc jockey called Lenny Detroit came across a set of compact discs, more challenging and abstract than most. He listened to them repeatedly and claimed to have discovered the secret of the Record Library.

He observed, reasonably enough, that all the recordings, that is all the guitar solos, in the Record Library were comprehensible in terms of the same elements: notes, intervals, rhythms, duration, harmonies, counterpoint and so on. However unusual or different the solos sounded, and even if they consciously avoided or excluded some of those elements, they could still be analysed and described in terms of them.

He also postulated that in the vastness of the library there were no two identical guitar solos. Since nobody had ever heard every disc in the library, not even visited every listening booth, this could not be proved, and yet there was something about the postulation that made sense and appealed.

From these two premises Detroit then deduced that the Record Library is total and that the compact discs within it contain all possible combinations of guitar-playing elements. In other words, the discs in the library contain everything that it is possible for the guitar to express. Everything.

Somewhere on disc in the infinite vastness of the Record Library is every guitar solo that ever has been or ever will be played: all the blues solos, all the jazz solos, all the country and western solos, all the rock and roll, all the mainstream and all the avant-garde, all the technically brilliant and all the totally incompetent. The library must contain all the great, pithy solos and all the tedious rambling ones, the self-indulgent as well as the finely honed, the deeply flawed as well as the nearly perfect, all the absolutely right notes and all the totally bum notes. Everything.

(Fandom is full of talk about solos being 'unbelievable', or 'incredible' or 'impossibly good', but the literally impossible is obviously excluded from the Record Library. On the other hand, it suffices only that a solo be possible for it to exist and be present.)

When the Detroit theory was proclaimed, the first reaction was one of extravagant happiness. All guitarists felt themselves to be masters of a secret treasure. They belonged to a great tradition. Their guitar solos, even the most modest of them, were part of the vital fabric of the universe. It felt good.

But, as was perhaps inevitable, this happiness was followed

by a general, universal depression. The certitude that some compact disc in some far distant listening booth already held every solo the guitarist was ever going to play seemed intolerable. What was the point in trying to be original or inventive or experimental, if the result was already foregone and foreknown? What was the point of perfecting new techniques or of trying to experiment?

Some suggested that all further attempts at inspiration or composition or improvisation should cease and that guitarists should simply juggle notes and chords at random, possibly using computers, until, by an improbable gift of chance, they created great guitar solos; although, of course, these solos too would already exist somewhere in the Record Library.

The belief that everything had already been played transformed some guitarists into phantoms. I know of listening booths where young men sit and listen to certain recordings over and over again, bow down before them, learn them note for note and say, 'We are not worthy'. They get into arguments, into fights. There are warring factions and fan clubs. There are even attempts to form 'tribute bands'.

Others said it was time to apply some quality control. What was the use, they insisted, of keeping solos that were hackneyed, repetitive or downright unlistenable? The Record Library, by definition, must contain much that was bad or second (indeed tenth) rate, and it therefore needed purifying. They started a secret campaign and managed to erase hundreds of hours of heavy metal guitar solos before their ruse was discovered. The damage they had done was, in the strictest sense, irreparable, but it could also be said that, given the size of the Record Library, the damage was infinitesimal. Certain solos had undoubtedly gone forever but, as is the way with heavy metal, there were plenty more where they'd come from.

So what are the consequences of this for someone like myself, a fanatical Jenny Slade enthusiast? I know that the Record Library must contain everything she ever has or ever will play. It must contain her greatest solos and her worst (although even at her worst I still find her guitar playing utterly compelling). I know it must also contain any number of variations on these solos; solos that in some cases must vary by just one note, or which are played at a minutely different tempo. The library must contain solos by other guitarists whose playing either accidentally or deliberately sounds like Jenny Slade. There will be imitations, parodies, pastiches of her work. Equally the library must contain solos that she would like to have played, that she might have played given enough time. It must also contain slightly improved and slightly worsened versions of each of her extant solos, although I would argue that much of her work is incapable of improvement.

There is another set of scholars I heard of recently who have begun a new enterprise within the listening booths. Somewhere in the Record Library, they reason, there must be one CD that contains better guitar solos than any of the other discs, a sort of greatest hits collection. Not only that, this disc would contain the essence and the heart of the whole Record Library and of the universe. They have searched for it for years, and they are still searching even now. They are supreme optimists, and their faith is touching.

Some say this is a foolish, even a dangerous enterprise. Some say the task is impossible because it relies too much on subjective matters; others say it is a sort of blasphemy, a challenge to

God and infinity. I recognize these problems, but in the end I think they're entirely solvable. I believe, indeed I would be prepared to say I *know*, that Jenny Slade is quite simply the best guitarist who's ever lived, who's ever going to live. The quintessential disc that these scholars seek would be identical to and synonymous with the best of Jenny Slade.

I realize I may be alone in this opinion but I have profound reasons for holding it and I truly believe that sooner or later the world will agree with me. My solitude is lightened by this elegant hope.

Reprinted from the *Journal of Sladean Studies*
Volume 2 Issue 6

'So what is that exactly?' Kate asks, when she's read the article.

'It's a post-modern appreciation of Jenny Slade,' says Bob humourlessly.

'Is it indeed?'

'Yes. It has to be. You see, Jenny Slade's not only the best guitarist in the world, she's also the most Po-Mo.'

Kate is a tad confused. Maybe Bob doesn't quite share her feelings about Jenny Slade. That needn't be so terrible, there are many different ways of appreciating something, yet she suspects that Bob would insist that his way is the only true path.

'You don't say,' Kate replies.

'I do,' says Bob. 'Really I do.'

The bar is all but empty. There's one drunk sleeping contentedly by the jukebox and the manager has gone, telling Kate to lock up when she's had enough of her new-found friend.

Kate says to Bob, 'I don't suppose you've got the time to explain post-modernism have you?'

Bob looks at his watch and shakes his head sadly.

'That's what they all say,' Kate complains.

'But I've still got plenty to tell you about Jenny Slade.'

Kate cheers up at this news.

'All right,' she says, 'you can tell me about post-modernism another time.'

The promise that she's prepared to spend 'another time' with him soothes Bob's wounded heart.

'Now I think we should talk about instrumentation,' he says.

LEMON-SQUEEZING TIME

A hot, humid bedroom in a shack in Greenwood, Mississippi, in August 1938; bare walls, bare floors, the cracked windows repaired with duct tape, a bed thin as a tortilla. It looks like ancient history, but it's not so long ago.

He's unsure how he got here. Maybe someone from the club brought him home when they saw just how sick he was. And still is. In this rare moment of sense and clarity he looks around the room, sees the empty moonshine bottle beside the bed, his own sharp suit and shiny shoes arranged on a chair like a wraith. No sign of his guitar.

The sheets are tangled and wet with sweat, and swathed in them is Robert Johnson, blues singer and guitarist. He's sick as a dog; pains in his head and stomach, in his very bones. In fact sometimes he *howls* like a dog, screams, sees visions, bays at invisible moons, talks to ghosts and demons. He hears music, not his own; strange stuff, from another country, or maybe another planet, like Mars or some such place.

It could all be worse. He could be in a tar-paper hut in the middle of a swamp somewhere. He could still be on the plantation, or being worked over by smiling deputies. Being able to sing and play guitar hasn't kept him out of trouble completely, hasn't made his life a breeze, but without his gift he knows that everything about his existence would have been twenty times worse.

But why exactly does he feel so bad? It was just another weekend gig. He sang and played just like usual. All he did different was take a drink of whisky, from a bottle given him by the club owner. The guy sure had a good-looking wife and she sure did flash a nice smile poor Bob's way, but he didn't do anything about it. There were nights when he would have done, but not tonight. And he certainly couldn't do anything once he'd started throwing up his guts. He certainly hadn't done anything that you'd poison a guy for. Was he being punished just for his thoughts?

And suddenly, oh shit, there's a woman in the room. Not the club owner's wife, much worse than that, much scarier: a white woman. He's in enough trouble already and this woman looks like really bad news. She's wearing the weirdest outfit he's ever seen, like fancy dress, like she's a show girl or a specialized kind of harlot maybe. It's pretty indecent the way her clothes hug her body, and show off her legs and breasts. She isn't strictly his type. He prefers something more homely, someone older and more comfortably reassuring, but he can definitely see the attraction. And although he doesn't exactly know how, there seems to be some sort of connection between this woman and the infernal outer-space music he keeps hearing.

That's when he realizes he must be hallucinating. Oh sure, she looks solid and real enough, as though you could reach out and grab yourself a handful, but he knows she must be the product of his sick imagination. What manner of woman would be here with him at a place and a time like this? What the hell was in that moonshine that created such visions?

'Hi, Robert,' she says.

'You know my name?' he asks, but then why should he be surprised? That's the way it is with hallucinations. They know everything.

'I know all about you,' she confirms.

'And who the hell are you?'

'I'm Jenny Slade.'

'And what do you want from me?' he asks.

'I don't want anything much. I just want to tell you about the future.'

'You mean I got one?' he says, as a stab of pain twangs through him.

'Well, yes and no. That moonshine whisky the bar owner gave you, I'm afraid it *is* going to kill you.'

'Oh Jesus.'

'But that's OK. That's not the end of the story.'

'No? It sure sounds like it to me.'

'No, you have posterity on your side.'

'Post what?'

Jenny smiles indulgently. She knows he's not as dumb as he's pretending.

'Fifty or sixty years from now you'll be known as the "King of the Delta Blues Singers",' she says.

'I sure don't feel like no king right now.'

'Maybe not, but that's what they're going to call you.'

'Who's going to call me that?'

'Blues fans, and record companies and journalists, and radio stations.'

'You mean white folks, yeah?'

'Mostly white folks, yes.'

'Well, I ain't prejudiced,' he says, and he laughs through his sickness and stomach pain. 'And what about my guitar playing?'

'You're going to be very popular for your guitar playing too.'

'Hell, lady, I don't see that I have to wait fifty, sixty years. I'm popular right now, you know. I recorded my song "Terraplane Blues", and it sold maybe five thousand copies. If that ain't popular then I don't know what is.'

'You're going to be even more popular than that.'

'For sure?'

'For sure,' she confirms.

Johnson doesn't seem inclined to believe her. He says, 'You see, these guys came down from the American Record Company. I recorded twenty-nine sides for 'em. I made big money out of it.'

'Big money for here and now, maybe.'

'Yeah, well here and now's where I'm at.'

'That's true, but things are going to change, Robert.'

He looks at her slyly, squinting through half-closed eyes.

'Hey,' he says. 'You ain't some kind of devil woman, are you? Come to take my soul away?'

'Is that what you think I am?'

'Well, no, can't really say that I do, but you sure are a weird one.'

She looks at him disapprovingly, like a school teacher

trying to chastise a pupil with a single look; an evil eye, maybe.

'What is it with you and the devil, Robert?'

'What you mean?'

'I mean all this stuff about having hellhounds on your trail and having Satan knock on your door. What's the point of all that?'

'Say, you must've heard me sing. You must've paid attention.'

'Yes,' she says patiently. 'I've heard you play many times, and I always wonder what's all this nonsense about you having made some sort of pact with the devil.'

'Hell, you don't have to believe that stuff,' Johnson says dismissively. 'It's just showbiz. I had a friend called Ike claimed he learned to play guitar by sitting in a graveyard, letting the knowledge seep up through the tombstones into his ass. I don't think too many folks believed him.'

'So you don't believe any of that stuff you peddle?'

'I don't believe in it exactly, but it does no harm to pay a bit of lip service, you know what I mean?'

'Are you sure it does no harm?' Jenny says, and she seems concerned. 'You see, it seems to me that all this stuff about being in league with the devil is more than just bullshit, Robert. It's actually very demeaning. It suggests that a poor black man couldn't possibly have genius unless it was somehow handed to him from an external source. And that's bad, Robert. That's absolute crap. They try to pull the same stuff with women. You aren't in touch with any devil, Robert, you're just in touch with yourself.'

'I'd sure like to get in touch with you,' he says.

102

It's a well-intentioned offer but they both know that Johnson's in no condition to go touching women. Jenny sits down on the edge of the bed, but she's visiting the sick, not accepting any sexual invitation.

'It's with the boys that you're really going to be a hit. You're going to be a big influence on lots of guys, a lot of them white.'

'Now I know I'm dreamin'.'

'There's going to be a guy called Eric who's going to base his whole career on playing "Crossroads". Of course, it won't sound much like your version; he'll garble the words a bit and take a verse from a different song, and he'll add a Chicago-style riff, but you'll get a lot of the credit for it.'

'And will I get money for it?'

'You won't need money when you're dead.'

'Yeah, but—'

'And a band named after an airship will take some of your best tunes and lines and make them their own. And there'll be books written about you, scholarly articles, television programmes, movies.'

It's all getting too much for him now. All these words and ideas that he doesn't quite understand.

'What are you?' he asks. 'A fortune teller?'

'No. And I'm not here just to tell you about your own future. I want to tell you about *everybody*'s future.'

'You sure are something. OK, go ahead, tell me about the future.'

'Well, the first thing is, the future's going to be very loud.'

'Guess I can live with that.'

'Louder than you ever imagined.'

'What? Like a thunder storm? Or a steam train?'

'Like a train going through a storm with bombs exploding all around it.'

'You mean there's going to be a war?'

'Well, as a matter of fact, there is, World War Two, but you needn't worry about that. You won't live to see it. But after the war everything will be different. The young people who missed it will want their music to sound as loud as a war.'

Johnson looks around again for his own scratched guitar, but it seems to have gone for good. He says, 'Then I guess there won't be much use for guitar pickers.'

Jenny laughs. 'There's going to be lots of use for guitar pickers, Robert. The word may not have got to Mississippi yet but there are already guys out there who are creating something called the electric guitar.'

'Yeah? Would that be anything like an electric chair?'

She smiles but presses on. 'You see there's this little thing called amplification. Imagine you plucked a guitar string and it made a noise like, oh I don't know, like a screaming banshee.'

'That'd be spooky.'

'That'll be standard, Robert. With an electric guitar and the right amplification you're going to be able to play to crowds of hundreds of thousands of people. And you're going to be able to change the way your guitar sounds. You'll be able to make it sound like you're playing in a big empty warehouse, or in a cave. And you'll be able to make it sound like a swarm of bees or a dynamite explosion.'

'Why in God's name would I want it to sound like a dynamite explosion?'

'Maybe you wouldn't, Robert, but believe me there'll be plenty of guitarists who will.'

'White folks?'

'No, not exclusively white folks.'

'You mean black folks are going to be able to afford these fancy electric things?'

'Oh yes,' she says. 'The electric guitar will be available to more or less anybody.'

'Well, that sounds like progress. And what'll this amplification stuff look like?'

'It'll be a box, just a little black box with a plug and a speaker.'

'Devil's boxes.'

'There you go again, Robert. And certain people will make music simply by ramming their guitars against these amplifiers. There'll be guys who smash up their guitars as part of the act.'

Johnson looks at her as though she's now telling the tallest of tall stories and has gone too far, passed the point of believability and sanity.

He says, 'I once had my guitar smashed up by a couple of good ol' southern boys. It didn't sound so good to me.'

'Well, it won't only be a question of the way it *sounds*.'

'Didn't look too pretty neither.'

'It's more a symbolic act, I guess,' she said.

'You sure do talk fancy. Are you foreign maybe? From somewhere like England? Or from some other planet? Some other time?'

'Sure,' she says. 'I'm all those things.'

'And that music I keep hearing. You responsible for that?'

'Yes, that's my music.'

'You a guitar player?'

'Definitely.'

'That's nice. I like a woman who knows how to hold down a chord.'

Jenny is relaxed and softer now, as though she's done what she came for, got over the important and difficult part of her visit. She asks, 'Have you got any advice for me about guitar playing?'

Johnson's face clouds over and he feels a twinge of pain rising and stabbing all the way from his stomach to his throat.

'Sure,' he says with difficulty. 'I got some advice for you. Next time you feel like going down to the crossroads – don't.'

He laughs until it hurts, then screeches with pain. The terrible sound brings a man running into the bedroom. It's Honeyboy Edwards, Johnson's good friend, the man who brought him here when he saw how ill he was. Johnson looks around him, thinking he has some explaining to do, about how he comes to have a white woman in his room. At the very least he thinks that he should make some introductions, but suddenly Jenny Slade is nowhere to be seen. The music has gone too, and so has the relief from pain that her presence seemed to bring.

'How ya feelin'?' Edwards asks.

Robert Johnson looks as though he's giving the question

some slow, serious consideration. Then he says, casual as you like, 'You know, Honeyboy, I do believe I'm sinkin' down.'

ONE HAND TAPPING

Audiences are strange things. Sometimes they can feel like one whole, living organism. Other times they are no more than a loose posse of separate, diverse, isolated individuals, with nothing at all in common, least of all a desire to see the act they happen to be watching.

Jenny Slade always liked to seek out the faces of one or two of her audience. It made the gig personal. It was a place to focus her energies. But usually that was all they were; faces. She didn't take in much about the owner of each face, couldn't have told you whether he or she was tall or short, old or young, how they were dressed, whether, for example, they were disabled.

It was November, and she had played a disappointing gig to a small, cold audience in a converted bus garage in South Yorkshire. Early on she'd looked out at the blank faces in search of a friend, someone warm and on her side. Sometimes, if she worked it right, that little centre of warmth could spread itself outwards and include the rest of the audience and bring them over to her, but on this occasion that had failed to happen. She'd found the face all right. It belonged to a young man with a shaved head and a big smile, and the smile had grown wider as the gig had gone on. He was obviously enjoying himself, but just as obviously he was in a minority, possibly a minority of one. By the end it seemed as though the whole gig had been directed solely at him.

Afterwards he was in the bar, on his own, and looking much younger than he had from the stage, barely into his teens, and though Jenny didn't make a habit of talking to strange young men in bars, especially not at her own gigs, she found herself saying to him, 'Thank God you were there.' And she tried to shake him by the hand but he made no attempt to reciprocate. He had a beer in his right hand and, as she suddenly saw, he had no left arm at all, just a jacket with a limp, empty right sleeve.

Jenny was duly embarrassed. She started to apologize, though that too was embarrassing and she knew she really had nothing to apologize for. The guy smiled and shrugged it off.

'These things happen,' he said, and he seemed to be referring to all sorts of things: to bad gigs, to the loss of limbs, to being socially embarrassed.

'They certainly do,' Jenny agreed, and that was the end of the conversation. But on the way back to her hotel she had a strange sense that there was something familiar about the boy, and though she had only the shakiest sense of there being anything meaningful about it, she got the curious feeling that she'd seen other one-armed boys at her gigs. She wasn't sure if that was odd or not. One-armed men could enjoy her music as much as anyone else, though clearly their personal knowledge of guitar playing would have to be mostly theoretical.

At the next gig, in a converted distillery in Fife, there was another one-armed boy in the audience, and then another when she played at a jam session in Camden. She didn't get to speak to either of them, but when she was coming out of a guitar shop in Denmark Street a few days later and saw yet another one-armed boy gazing longingly at the second-hand Strats and Les Pauls in the window, she knew she had to talk. She stood next to him and joined him in looking.

'Nice guitars,' she said.

'I'll say,' the boy agreed and he smiled broadly at her, just the way the first guy had. There was something not quite right about that smile. It was a little too serene for Jenny's tastes.

She noticed that the boy was wearing a lapel badge. The letters SOFT were set in blue enamel against a red background littered with stars. And she remembered the first boy had also been wearing such a badge.

'Is SOFT the name of a band?' she asked.

'No,' the boy replied. 'It stands for Sons of Freddie Terrano.'

'Freddie Terrano?' she said. It was a name she hadn't heard in two decades. 'Whatever happened to him?'

'Oh, things,' he said, and he smiled again, shrugged philosophically and slouched off. If he knew what had happened to Freddie Terrano, and since he was wearing the badge she assumed he did, then he certainly wasn't telling.

Freddie Terrano, almost certainly not his real name, was one of those people who had found the guitar an almost laughably easy instrument to play. He could have been a great jazz player, an authentic bluesman, a classical soloist, just about anything he wanted. But he'd made his reputation as that most peculiar of all phenomena, the lead guitarist in a glam rock band called the Beams. In interviews he'd talked of wanting to write symphonies for guitar orchestras. He quoted Guitar Slim and Debussy and Adorno; but when he got on stage he played loud, bludgeoning pentatonic rock over a leaden 4/4 beat created by the band's two drummers.

The Beams made two successful albums and could no doubt have continued forever, playing revival tours and the supper-club circuits, but everybody knew Freddie Terrano was made for something better. He signed a solo deal and the Beams split up in a round of legal actions about who was entitled to use the name.

For a while Freddie Terrano's solo album was 'eagerly awaited' and then it was 'long delayed' and shortly after that nobody was waiting for it at all. The moment had been ripe, but the moment passed. The solo album never appeared. Those who still thought about Freddie Terrano at all, and few did, assumed he had blown it by one method or another; too many drugs, too little inspiration, too much fear of putting his money where his mouth was. His continuing silence gave him a certain mystique but Jenny still thought Freddie Terrano was an odd figure to have any badge-wearing 'sons'.

Not having given Freddie Terrano a moment's thought in twenty years, she found herself thinking about him all the time. She dug out her old Beams records and it was weird, yes, the guitarist was pretty good, but it seemed as though he was doing his damnedest to hide the fact. The question of Freddie Terrano's fate became extraordinarily pressing. There were other questions too.

Finally, at a gig in a converted army barracks in Aldershot, she cornered yet another one-armed boy with a SOFT badge on his jacket and demanded, 'What is it with you guys? Why do you Sons of Freddie Terrano keep turning up at my gigs?'

The boy was terrified to find himself being interrogated by the artist he'd come to see, but he sounded like he was telling the truth when he said, 'Because Freddie tells us to.'

'What do you mean, he tells you to?' Jenny asked.

'You know, we go to his place and we discuss things and he tells us you're pretty good.'

'You go to his place?'

'Sure. You want me to get you an invitation?'

Jenny found it strange to think that a man she hadn't given a thought to in twenty years was out there recommending her, gaining her an audience. She could use all the audience she could get, but it was still strange.

'What happened to your arm?' she asked the boy bluntly.

'It's gone. These things happen.'

'How do you mean? Where did it go? How? Why? When?'

She could see him struggling with himself; should he tell her or not? He decided he would.

'OK,' he said. 'I did it myself.'

'Yourself?'

'I did it for Freddie. So I could be like him.'

'What? You mean Freddie Terrano only has one arm?'

'You're really out of touch, aren't you, Miss Slade?'

'Apparently.'

'That was why he never made his solo album.'

'Yes, well, I can see it would have slowed him down.'

'We SOFTs, as we like to call ourselves, chop off our arms so we can be in his image. It wasn't so hard. I like to think of it as body sculpture. Some people have cosmetic surgery; we go for this. It's no different.'

'Oh, I think it is,' Jenny said gruffly. 'I really do think it is. Does Freddie Terrano know what you've done in his name?'

'Sure.'

'And how does he feel about it?'

'Well, you know, he's a cool guy. I guess he's pleased to have such loyal fans.'

Now she couldn't think about anything other than Freddie Terrano and his little band of self-mutilated fans. Even when she was sitting at home slouched in front of the TV screen, practising guitar while watching reruns of *The Fugitive*, she couldn't get rid of his ugly sinister presence. When the phone call came it was something of a relief.

'Hello,' said a deep, slightly American-stained voice. 'This is Freddie Terrano. It's time we met.'

He sounded eager and Jenny wanted to meet him at least as much as he wanted to meet her. He said he'd send a car for her, and sure enough a car arrived, but it wasn't some luxurious stretch limo, just a beat-up old jalopy with a series of spider cracks across the windscreen and a driver who wore a World War One tin hat and favoured an almost horizontal driving position.

The drive was a short one and when the car stopped and the driver made a big number out of opening the door for her, she was standing outside the steps of a small private hotel. A skinhead doorman in a burgundy uniform welcomed her and said that Mr Terrano was waiting for her in the bar, and he pointed her towards a flight of descending stairs.

The bar was small and dark and lit with candles. The walls were decorated with mirror fragments and mosaics. At first the place looked totally empty but then Jenny saw that a corner booth was occupied by a man who had his back to the centre of the room. He didn't turn even as Jenny approached the table, so that she had to walk right up to him before she could be certain it really was Freddie Terrano.

He looked younger than she'd expected. The last picture she'd seen of him showed him with exotic quiff and sideburns, dressed in metallic dungarees with eighteen-inch epaulets. The man in front of her looked sophisticated, knowing, and yes, as the young fan had said, very, very cool. He motioned for her to sit down and he leaned over, kissed her on the cheek and poured her a glass of something fierce and highly coloured from a pitcher that he'd already started on.

'Jenny,' he said. 'Good to see you at long last. You'll forgive me if I don't shake hands.'

And there it was, just as expected, the left sleeve of his jacket hanging empty by his body.

'How long is "at long last"?' she asked.

'What?'

'I mean, I'm surprised that you even know I exist. I was wondering how long you've been wanting to meet me, because frankly I'm not that hard to meet.'

114

'No need to be spiky,' he said, and she felt a little guilty, but only a little, and then she found herself staring at the empty sleeve and felt worse, but Freddie Terrano just smiled.

'I realize you'll want the full explanation,' he said. 'Although, frankly, there are times when I don't really understand it myself. It was such a long time ago, and sometimes I feel as though I wasn't even there.'

He recapped on his career with the Beams, right up to the moment when he was due to make his solo album.

'The studio time was booked, the producer was booked, the other musicians were booked; the only problem was I didn't know what the fuck I was going to do with this studio time and all these great musicians. I didn't have any songs, any material. Nothing.

'The record company didn't give a shit. They said, just turn up at the studio on the appointed day with my guitar and amp. All I had to do was crank up and show off. Whether it was jamming or cover versions or pure improvisation, didn't matter, they'd do whatever was required to turn it into a record. But it didn't seem right to me. I wanted some tunes, some melodies, some "proper" compositions. The problem was, I couldn't write any while I was at home.

'So I went off to Wales for a couple of weeks with my guitar and a big pad of manuscript paper. I rented a farm cottage and I was all set to get my act together. But I was every bit as uninspired in the country as I had been at home. Oh sure I could play blinding twenty-minute guitar solos, but that was no good, that was far too easy. I spent my days walking round the farm, and my nights getting blitzed on the stash of bad chemicals I'd brought along with me.

115

'By the end of the first week I was raging with boredom, but I'd got quite friendly with the farmer who owned the cottage and he suggested that some hard physical effort might be just what was needed to clear out the cobwebs. There was an old orchard that had been damaged by storms, fallen trees that needed sawing and clearing. He asked if I knew how to use a chainsaw, and I said sure.

'Well, you can probably guess the rest. I was lying to the farmer. I didn't know one end of a chainsaw from the other. I was hacking away at the trunk of some old apple trees when the chainsaw flew out of control and sawed off my left arm just a couple of inches below the shoulder. It was a mess.

'We leapt in the farmer's Land Rover and went to the hospital, me carrying my left arm in my right hand. The farmer was full of confidence that everything would be all right. He'd had a farm labourer a few years back who cut off his foot and they'd been able to sew it back on so you hardly knew it had been missing.

'But his confidence was misplaced. At the hospital they told me an arm was a very different proposition from a foot. They said they could sew the arm back on but there was no way it would ever be usable. I replied that if it wasn't going to be usable, then I didn't want the damn thing at all, and I wouldn't let them sew it back on. It was an unusual decision maybe, but that was how I felt.

'We kept it out of the papers. I didn't want sympathy. I didn't want to be the legendary one-armed axeman of rock, so I slipped away, abandoned my career, let it all die.

'For years I used to agonize about it. What if I hadn't left the Beams? What if I hadn't taken that holiday? What if I hadn't gone to help the farmer? What if I'd asked him to show me how to use a chainsaw?

'I think it was Jon Churchill, the drummer, a guy I'd met doing session work, who first came up with the theory that I'd done it on purpose. He said I'd always been an arrogant, big-headed shit. Everything had always been too easy for me. What most people take years to learn I could accomplish with one hand tied behind my back. I thought any damn fool could play a great guitar solo, whereas obviously it took a special kind of genius to saw off your own fretting arm. Maybe Churchill was right. How can you prove it either way? Or maybe I was just scared of making a lousy solo album.

'Of course, I wasn't exactly happy about it. When the initial trauma was over I realized that a large part of me still wanted to play the guitar. So for a while I messed around with prosthetics, and slides and open tunings and Van Halen-style tapping, but it wasn't the same. So then I thought about becoming a keyboard player, and I saw that with the use of synthesizers and foot pedals all sorts of things were possible, but frankly I wasn't good enough. I was a killer guitarist but I was only a very run-of-the-mill synth player. I think I wanted to be somewhere in between. I gave up music completely. That was no good either.

'Years passed. I didn't feel good but I felt OK. What was done was done, and then, you know how it is, everything gets recycled. Albums that were virtually impossible to get hold of when they were first released are now on sale in every Megastore. Things get remastered, remixed, repackaged.

Before you know where you are the Beams records are on CD and there's a brand new generation buying and liking them. Suddenly I started getting fan mail again, for fuck's sake. And every now and then somebody would track me down, think he was making a big "discovery", ask me was I still playing. Some of these "fans" would turn out to be A&R men for record companies, who thought maybe I was ripe for a comeback and they'd invite me to lunch where I'd show them my missing arm and they'd decide my comeback might have to be postponed for a while yet.'

'And then of course there are the boys from SOFT,' Jenny said sternly.

'SOFT has nothing to do with me,' Terrano said vehemently. 'I mean, they took my name, but I never asked them to. It started with a kid called Kenny Stevens. He was a young fan, a talented would-be rock guitarist. He could play every note on the two Beams albums. He worshipped me, perhaps a little too much. He knew nothing about my missing arm, of course, and he turned up on my doorstep one day saying he wanted to have a jam session with me. Then he saw that I only had one arm and he was devastated. He went away and the next thing I knew he'd sawn off his own arm, as a tribute to me. And believe it or not *he* found some followers, some like-minded Freddie Terrano fans. That's who the Sons of Freddie Terrano are, a bunch of fans who've mutilated themselves in my honour.'

'And do you feel honoured?'

'I'm not sure. I certainly feel flattered. You know, imitation is the sincerest form of fandom.'

'Why don't you try to stop them?'

'How can you stop young boys doing what they want to do?'

'Quite easily if you're one of their heroes,' Jenny said. 'You tell them not to do it, and because they want to honour you, they do what you tell them.'

Terrano didn't reply, but she could see that there was a whole part of him that was really getting off on the fact that young men were mutilating themselves into his image. She was disgusted.

'You are one sick fuck, Freddie Terrano,' she said.

'Hey, it's only rock and roll.'

'No, it's more than that,' Jenny insisted, and she stood up to leave.

'Hey, where are you going?'

'I don't want to sit here drinking with someone who encourages impressionable young guys to cut their arms off.'

'Hey, calm down,' Terrano said. 'There's lots I still have to say to you. I have a proposition.'

'I don't think so,' said Jenny, and she left the bar. The car was still waiting outside but she headed off in the other direction and she was not followed.

She went home, got on with her life, and tried hard not to think about Freddie Terrano and his followers, but it didn't work. She kept feeling she ought to do something about it, and she did deliver a small tirade on the subject at a gig in a converted boathouse in Lowestoft, but nobody seemed to know what she was talking about. It was true enough that the boys were free agents, and it was even possibly true that Freddie Terrano would have been powerless to stop them harming themselves, but Jenny thought he had a duty to try. It occurred to her that she should have stayed in the hotel bar that night and tried harder to convince him.

So when Freddie Terrano called again and was full of apologies, saying how sorry he was that they'd 'misunderstood' each other, she didn't immediately hang up. And when he said he wanted to meet again, she felt she had to go along with it, solely in the hope of getting him to change his mind and maybe save the arms of a few potential Freddie Terrano fans.

He sent the car as before, but this time it didn't take her to the neutral ground of a hotel bar. It took her to a wild, deserted part of town, a place of motorway flyovers and electrical component factories and breakers' yards, and specifically to an abandoned tower block, forty empty stories of decaying concrete and boarded-up windows. The car found a gap in the metal fence surrounding the base of the tower and went down a ramp into a service area where the building's innards still seemed to be in working order. There were overhead lights, the sound of running water, plumes of steam escaping from heating pipes.

The driver opened the car door for her as before and she stepped out, shivering not so much with cold as with foreboding. Freddie Terrano appeared from nowhere and beckoned for her to follow him. Having no choice, she did so, and was led into a huge void of what might once have been an underground car-park. There were concrete pillars at regular intervals and no walls subdivided the space. Freddie Terrano, however, had done his best to make the place look homely. Scattered, apparently at random, throughout were dozens, perhaps scores, of old settees and armchairs, no doubt the jetsam that had been left behind when the tower block was emptied. There were a number of coffee tables and side tables set in front of each settee, and beside or on top of each one was a standard or table lamp.

Then, in a not too distant recess of the basement Jenny saw something quite out of place, a beautiful Gretsch Astro-jet and an Electromatic Deluxe amp, the one with the bull's head printed on the speaker cloth. They looked as though they were in fantastic condition, as though they were just begging to be played. And although this wasn't just a social call, when Freddie Terrano said, 'Go ahead, play it for me, there's no way I can play it for myself,' there was no way she could resist.

She kept it simple, a melancholy tune, half strummed, half picked, an old thing of hers based on a lute composition by John Dowland. She was a little nervous and didn't play with quite as much heart or feeling as she would have liked, but when she was part-way through the piece she looked up and saw Freddie Terrano wiping tears from his eyes, and by the time she'd finished he was sitting on a beaten-up old sofa, with his head in his hand, his shoulders pulsing with a sadness that was for the world as well as for himself.

Ah well, Jenny thought, a man who is moved by your art, a man who cries when you play for him, can't be all bad. As she carefully put down the guitar she was aware that Freddie was rapidly trying to pull himself together.

'Forgive me,' he said.

'There's nothing to forgive,' Jenny said, but then she wasn't sure that she really meant it. 'Now about these boys,' she added brusquely.

'Not again,' said Terrano.

'Yes, again,' she insisted. 'Don't you think you have a duty to stop these young men ruining their lives?'

'How are their lives ruined?'

'Well, they can't play the guitar for one thing.'

'The fewer people play the guitar, the better,' he said. 'Guitar playing has never brought me anything other than pain and despair.'

'Well, for some people it's a joy.'

'Only very shallow people,' Freddie insisted.

'And anyway, it's not just guitar playing. Having only one arm must make plenty of other things more difficult too; things like eating, getting dressed, driving, sex.'

He laughed at her viciously.

'What would you know about it?' he asked. 'The fact is, my sex life got about five hundred per cent better the moment I lost my arm. There are a million reasons why women have sex with men, but sympathy and curiosity are very high on the list, and a one-armed man rates high on both those items.'

'I never thought about it that way,' Jenny admitted.

'Maybe you never thought about it at all,' Freddie said.

That quietened her. She accepted a beer as a sort of peace offering, but she was not accepting defeat.

'I didn't bring you here to argue. I actually have something to ask you,' Terrano said, sounding unusually hesitant. 'There's something I'd like you to try for me on guitar.'

'All right, what do you want me to play?'

He looked infinitely sheepish and said, 'A duet.'

Jenny was puzzled and felt very stupid. She had no idea what he could be wanting.

'Let me explain,' he said. 'We'll play a duet on the same guitar. I want you to play the neck with your left hand, and I'll pluck the strings with my right. We'll just improvise, see what comes out.'

She felt moved and she agreed readily enough. It didn't seem so very much to ask. The playing was awkward at first. Simply finding a position from which they could both reach the guitar was difficult enough, the business of co-ordinating the fretting and the picking was harder still. But after fifteen minutes or so they began to get used to each other's technique. He could anticipate when she was about to make a chord change, while she in turn began to respond to the different picking styles he used. The music came slowly, it was sometimes tentative and it was always a little edgy, but it wasn't at all bad.

'Yes,' Freddie said. 'Yes, I thought it would work. I heard some of your records, I really admired your left-hand technique. I knew we could do something together.'

It was tiring to play in this odd manner, and before long they'd both had enough. The guitar was put aside and they began to talk. Freddie Terrano wasn't at all the ogre that Jenny had first expected, and she found it almost impossible to believe he was willing to let young men slice themselves up in his name.

A week later Jenny Slade returned for more of the same, and before long it had turned into a regular weekly gig. If she didn't have a booking then Tuesday nights would always find her down in Freddie Terrano's underground car-park, moving her left hand up and down the neck of the Gretsch, while Freddie plucked or picked or strummed. Before long they became extremely skilled at reacting quickly and intuitively to each other's musical ideas. They sounded good. If someone had simply heard the music without seeing the physical circumstances of how the music was made, it would have been easy to believe there was only one person playing. However, a more experienced listener, one who'd heard enough of both Jenny Slade and Freddie Terrano, would have been amazed, and perhaps delighted, to find that the newly improvised music sounded simultaneously like both guitarists, and not simply a combination of both player's quirks or trademarks, but a true amalgam that contained all their best qualities.

Each Tuesday they played, and afterwards they talked and drank and sometimes smoked a few spliffs, and a little after midnight Jenny would go home. It became one of her favourite dates. Playing for no money to no audience was more satisfying than many of her paying gigs. After a while, however, Freddie insisted on recording their sessions, nothing fancy, just a single mike hooked up to a slightly decrepit cassette machine. Jenny wasn't sure that was in the true spirit of their improvisations but she didn't argue. Freddie joked that he only wanted the recordings so he could listen to his own mistakes, but in truth there were very few of those. Jenny recognized that she and Freddie Terrano had something special, a true empathy, a genuine musical connection. She didn't know where it was going or whether it had a future, but she recognized that much of the best music leads nowhere and exists only in the present.

When she arrived one Tuesday night she knew something was wrong. She entered Freddie's basement and saw the guitar was lying face down on the concrete floor with several of its strings broken. She couldn't see Freddie at first but that was because he was flat on his back on one of the many sofas. Eventually he realized she was there and made a bold attempt to stand up, but he wasn't very convincing. His legs swayed like palm trees in a hurricane and the bottle of vodka in his hand swung in counterpoint. There was a dull but dangerous expression in his eyes and there was a pile of tape cassettes at his feet, the ones he'd made of their duets, and as he walked towards her he trod on several of them. Jenny heard the brittle crack of plastic, of cassettes being split open. But Freddie never quite made it over to where she was standing. On the way there his legs gave out and he let gravity lay him out on a long lime-green sofa.

'What's up?' Jenny asked.

Freddie shook his head theatrically, as though he didn't want to talk about it, yet it was obvious that he did, obvious too that Jenny would have to go through the performance of pretending to drag it out of him against his will. When this had been gone through he pointed at the tapes on the floor.

'I did a daft thing,' he said. 'I played them to an A&R guy I know. I thought we had the makings of a decent album.'

'I take it he didn't like them,' Jenny said.

Freddie Terrano swigged the vodka. 'That's right. He

125

reckoned they were OK but they were a bit boring. He said I needed a gimmick.'

Terrano laughed so loud, so hard, so bitterly, that Jenny found herself joining in his derision.

'Having one arm wasn't gimmick enough. So I'm drinking again,' he said. 'Drinking being one of those things you can do on your own with only one hand.'

Jenny sat down on the edge of the sofa and said she'd be happy to help him drown his sorrows. He handed her the bottle and the next couple of hours passed rapidly as she and Freddie discussed the various evils of the music biz and all its personnel.

As the alcohol kicked in, Jenny's feelings for Freddie got much warmer. Once she'd thought he was a monster, but now she felt protective towards him. She understood his hurt and disappointment. She felt sympathy, and yes, maybe she was a little curious sexually. She thought this was probably going to be the night she slept with Freddie Terrano. She leaned against him on the sofa. She closed her eyes and the world became a swimming, buzzing, hurtling place. She needed Freddie's arms around her, to steady her, to steady the room. But Freddie was no longer beside her. She opened her eyes and saw he was standing a few yards away, looking perfectly steady now as though he'd drunk himself back to sobriety. At first she thought he was holding a guitar in his hand, something yellow and black and weirdly shaped.

'You know what else the A&R man said to me?' Freddie blustered. 'He said what would really make for a great act would be if we were *both* one-armed; two one-armed guitarists playing a single guitar. He said he'd sign up an act like that straight away. The fact that you had two arms was a problem. As far as he was concerned, Jenny, you have one arm too many.'

And then Jenny was in no doubt about what Freddie Terrano had in his hand. It wasn't a guitar at all. It was a chainsaw.

'Come on, Jenny,' he said. 'We all have to make sacrifices for the sake of our careers.'

'You're out of your mind,' Jenny said.

'Of course I'm out of my mind,' Freddie raged. 'If you'd lost an arm, spent twenty years in the wilderness, finally found a way to make music and then had some record company hack dismiss it like that, you'd be out of your mind too.'

Jenny could see there was a lot of truth in this, but that didn't make the chainsaw look any less threatening. Freddie Terrano pressed the starter and the machine seethed into life.

'Like I told you, life with one arm isn't so bad,' Freddie insisted. 'For one thing you'll have a whole new set of fans. You can start a fan club called the Daughters of Jenny Slade.'

He danced across the floor and slashed at the first thing he saw, a leatherette winged chair, cutting it open in a burst of stuffing and sawdust.

'But supposing we did both have one arm,' Jenny said, for one moment considering the terrible prospect, 'what would we be? Nobody would ever take us seriously. We'd be a novelty act, a freak show.'

'And what kind of an act am I now?' he asked.

He brandished the chainsaw again and whacked it against

one of the concrete pillars. Sparks flew and he bounced away like a pinball.

'Look,' Jenny pleaded, 'even if, God help us, you succeed in hacking my arm off, how can you possibly think that after that I'd agree to form an act with you?'

'What other choice would you have?'

'I'd find some other way to play.'

'Oh really? Like *I* did?'

He advanced on her. She looked around for something to defend herself with and the only thing that came to hand was the guitar, the classic Gretsch Astrojet. She grabbed it, held the body towards her, the neck sticking out like a lance. It wasn't much defence against a chainsaw, but it was such a beautiful piece of work that she hoped Freddie would think twice before destroying it.

He didn't. He brought the saw round in a big curve and sawed through the neck where it joined the body. He was now within easy striking distance of Jenny. One lucky or highly skilled stroke and he could mutilate her to his preferred design. The smell of petrol from the saw made her nauseous, the noise of the chain filled her head so she couldn't think, and maybe that was why neither she nor Freddie Terrano heard the approaching footsteps, and why they barely heard the young male voice shout, 'Put that chainsaw down or I'll brain you.'

Freddie Terrano turned slowly round to see six young one-armed men standing in a semi-circle by the entrance to the basement. None of them was smiling. Between them they were carrying a huge scaffolding pole and there was no doubt they intended to use it.

'Put it down, Freddie, it's all over,' said the young man again.

Freddie looked at the chainsaw in his hand as though seeing it for the first time, as though it had somehow crawled there unbidden. He turned off the motor and set it down on the floor, and he looked at the young man who'd spoken. It was someone he recognized, Kenny Stevens, the first of his 'sons'.

'*Et tu*, Kenny?' he asked.

'*Moi*, above all,' Kenny replied, and he turned to Jenny and said, 'I owe you a big thank you, Ms Slade. I was there at the gig in Lowestoft when you spoke out against Freddie Terrano. You wouldn't have seen me, I was just one more face in the crowd, but you really set me thinking.'

'Thank God,' Jenny said.

Kenny Stevens picked up the abandoned chainsaw and cradled it in the bend of his right arm.

'I called a meeting,' he continued, 'and we Sons of Freddie Terrano have done some rapid growing up. I mean, everybody does stupid things when they're young, but hacking off your left arm, that's the stupidest of all.'

'No,' said Freddie softly, 'it wasn't stupid. It was very brave, very moving.'

'And you encouraged us, Freddie. You egged us on.'

'Did I? Well, even if I did, I can make stupid mistakes too, can't I?'

'We realize, of course, that nothing we do can ever give us our arms back, but we've also realized there's something we could do that would make us all feel a lot better.'

Freddie Terrano's face became hot and rigid as he watched

Kenny Stevens bring the chainsaw back to life. Jenny's own face, indeed her whole body, became equally inert. She knew she couldn't interfere. She could only stand by, her head down, her eyes turned away, as Freddie Terrano was reduced from a man with one arm to a man with none.

'Don't worry, Ms Slade,' Stevens said. 'You were never here. You never saw or heard anything. The name Freddie Terrano, the initials SOFT, they mean nothing to you, right?'

'Right,' Jenny agreed and she hurried away, all her senses gone horribly dead.

Later she worried about the tapes she and Freddie had made, that had been played to the A&R man, then trampled underfoot. Were they enough to connect her to the scene of the crime? If Freddie Terrano decided to squeal, she was anything but an innocent party. But time went by and the police never came knocking on her door, no investigative journalist ever came snooping around. The episode was closed. However, perhaps as a consequence of that night, one-armed boys stopped attending her gigs. She looked for them, she almost wanted to see them again, but they never reappeared.

Years later she did hear that bootlegs of the Slade/Terrano collaborations were obtainable if you were prepared to go to a little trouble. Generally it involved meeting a one-armed man in some weird and dangerous location, late at night, and handing over a lot of cash. Jenny didn't mind too much. How else were the poor Sons of Freddie Terrano supposed to make a living? And as for Freddie Terrano himself, one rumour said that he was alive and well and had started a new career in Egypt working as a glitter-clad novelty tap dancer on Nile cruises. It might have been true but Jenny preferred not to believe it.

PERFORMANCE NOTES

Bob Arnold reviews a Jenny Slade gig to cherish

The Psychology Club takes place on alternate Thursdays in a disused missile silo in Kent. Audiences are small but discerning. Improvisation is the name of the game; improvisation along with subversion, aural mayhem and cheap guitar thrills.

Last Thursday Tom Scorn and Jenny Slade premièred a new untitled piece, a work for computer, voice and guitar. There was talk that the pair had fallen out in the past over artistic differences, but on this occasion the hatchet seemed to be well and truly buried.

Scorn has always been as much into language as music, and on this occasion he vocalized while Jenny played her flesh guitar. In front of Scorn was a small computer programmed to create an endless stream of words and phrases, maybe even whole sentences, but using only the letters ABCDEF and G – the letters that correspond to the notes of western music. Sharps and flats were out. Scorn was to shout out this computer-generated language and Jenny would play their musical equivalents.

Jenny was free to choose where on the neck of the guitar and in which octave to play the notes. She was also free to decide whether notes were to be plucked, hammered on, pulled off, or played as harmonics. She could also determine the length of the notes, the time signature if appropriate, the degree of attack or sustain, the tone of the guitar, the effects used.

Simple words were obviously easy enough to translate into music notes, words like 'dad' and 'bed'. But some of the longer configurations would clearly be trickier, not only remembering and playing the notes, but also trying instantly to give the notes an intonation, a meaning that corresponded to the content of the language. Fortunately Jenny has always liked a challenge.

The audience settled, the lights went down and Tom Scorn tapped his computer. He peered at the tiny screen for a moment and then started. It was simple enough at first, just shouting out a few apparently random words. 'Egad,' he shouted. 'Gee! Ace! Fab!'

Jenny played the corresponding notes. Then it got a little tougher.

Perhaps remembering his art school background Scorn was heard to shout, 'Dada! Dada! Dada! Dada!'

Jenny played right along, and then it was as though Scorn were ordering food.

'Egg!' he shouted. 'Egg! Cabbage! Egg!'

A misty incomprehension settled over the audience, so Scorn addressed them directly. 'Deaf?' he enquired of several members of the front row. 'Deaf? Deaf?' and of the last person, 'Dead?'

And then he and the computer were off on a continuous, if only intermittently coherent, narrative.

'A café. A faded facade. Ed, a cad, cadged a fag. Ada, a deb, faced a bad decade. Bea, a babe, gagged. Abe bagged a cab.'

And then Scorn, or at least the computer, loosened up no

133

end, and the language became, not gibberish exactly, and not meaningless either, but Scorn found himself calling a long stream of unconnected words.

'Abba!' he shouted. 'Baa baa. Abed. Abba. Baggage. *Fad* baggage! A gaff? A badge? AC/DC. Gaga! Gaga! Gaga!'

Jenny was clearly doing her best to keep up with Scorn and yet not overtake him. It must have been all too tempting just to let her fingers do the walking and find that she had fallen into cliché, that she was playing some old blues riff.

And then something went terribly wrong with Scorn's computer. The cybernetic needle got stuck and for the next fifteen minutes or so all it came up with was 'gabba gabba gabba gabba gabba gabba'. The audience became restless. Ever the situationist, Scorn went with the flow and kept shouting the repeated word. Jenny, changing her guitar tone to something raw and fuzzed, had little choice but to follow where he led.

The audience reacted powerfully. Some said it was a superb piece of minimalism. Some said it was like being at a really bad Ramones gig. Others said there was no difference between these two propositions. Who knows how long the piece might have gone on if an audience member, a frail teenager in a gingham dress and flying helmet, fearing for her ears and/ or her sanity, hadn't leapt on stage and unplugged Scorn's computer?

Scorn was outraged and shouted many words that contained letters other than A to G, and stormed from the stage in a queeny fit. Jenny took off her guitar, cocked the tremolo arm, and left it to howl against the speaker, where the feedback note produced was a microtone pitched superbly between G and G#. It was a transcendent moment, one that is unlikely to be repeated in the near future.

Reprinted from the *Journal of Sladean Studies*
Volume 6 Issue 2

GROUPIE GUY

Nobody ever had to explain to Jenny Slade the sexual significance and symbolism of the electric guitar. She always knew it was a sexy instrument to touch and to look at, being simultaneously curvy and phallic. But for Jenny it was more than that. It was also a question of language, of vocabulary.

First, there was all that predictable dirty talk about fuzz boxes and truss rods, and 'spanking the plank' as a euphemism for guitar playing.

Then there were also all those sexy effects: compressors and enhancers, sustainers and flangers. It sounded as though there was a whole world of erotic possibilities among the pitch shifters, swell pedals, digital delays, and something excitingly clandestine in a noise suppressor. There was overdrive and treble boost. There were controls to modify presence, texture, gain, timbre, load impedance. Even a simple change in 'volume' could sound like a sexy concept if you were in the right mood.

But sex was one thing, love another. Had Jenny Slade ever known true love? (If it's not true then presumably it's not love.) Had she ever known that feeling they celebrate in popular song? She would have said yes, of course, and who was in any position to argue with her?

She understood the uneasy commerce between 'real' feelings and the sort people sing about; the description and the prescription. She knew that love songs don't merely describe the things we feel, they also sanction those things which we are capable of feeling. Did anyone ever think all they needed was love until the Beatles told them so? Did they know love was the drug, was blue, or that it came in spurts?

It seemed to her that popular music was best at describing and evoking certain kinds of lust and certain kinds of pain. It did it efficiently, in no time at all. Nobody ever needed a rock opera to say I want you, or I miss you.

Not that this compendium of feeling was necessarily unsophisticated. It asserted, rightly enough, that there are many chapters in the book of love. Yet it seemed to Jenny there were limits. Where was the song that would describe precisely what she had on her mind? It would have to say that she loved sex, was not naturally promiscuous although well aware of its attractions. There'd have to be a verse that said she was open to serious offers but that she feared submitting herself to another person since that other person would make impossible demands on her, would come between her and her guitar playing. And there would have to be a middle eight that compared the horrors of love gone wrong with the horrors of loneliness. Or was she wanting too much, being unnecessarily specific? Was it perhaps only the Everly Brothers she needed? Say 'Love Hurts' and leave it at that.

She wouldn't have claimed that she had searched

unusually long and hard for love, but she had always been alert, she'd always kept an eye open. She was not exactly sure where love and its triggers were to be found: in a body, yes, of course, and in a mind, in an ability to play a musical instrument, and in an attitude, in a certain way of standing on stage, of talking to an audience. Naturally she'd felt the seductiveness of other musicians, their ability to create a beauty that was not quite theirs, that was greater than them. But male musicians were ultimately depressing, too much to prove to themselves and to everyone else. Some of the female ones were a little better. She'd had exciting times with the lead singer of an all-female country and western band, who went so far as to write a song called 'You Went And Made A Lesbian Outa Me', but that wasn't the real thing either.

Undoubtedly there was such a thing as rock and roll sex, up tempo, with a back beat, with elements of thrash, in what looked like fancy dress; the familiar items of stage gear, leather jackets, leather trousers, leather bras. Perhaps it was best performed in transitive spaces, dressing rooms, hotel rooms, in the back of limos or vans. Drink and drugs were probably required, music turned up to the point of inaudibility, ideally a tape hot from the mixing desk. And then some paraphernalia, Polaroids, Handicams, silk ropes, plain and fancy sex aids. And maybe it needed more than two players so that it became a group experience, a band experience to be shared with a good number of participants and onlookers. Jenny had been some way down that road but turned back before the end of the cul-de-sac.

And yet alongside this there remained an innocence, or

at least a naivety, a youthfulness, a belief that love rejuven-
ated, that however many miles we have on the clock we're
still like teenagers (if not exactly like virgins) when we fall
in love (again) with love again, even if we never wanted to.

Or was Jenny's problem simply that she wasn't a singer?
She didn't use words, her own or other people's. She was
an instrumentalist and therefore what she expressed was
both too abstract and too particular to be reduced to a simple
message of love. Her music had 'meaning' but it wasn't language based. It might convey or recreate or even induce
certain feelings in the listener, and those might be erotic,
but there was never any narrative element, no story. Could
a guitar solo ever convey the same meaning as 'Why Do
Fools Fall In Love', or even as 'Wooden Heart'?

Wasn't art supposed to be comforting and consoling? Just
like love?

He went by the name of Jackie Brando and something clicked
for Jenny the moment she saw him. As was often the case
with one sort of music fan, he looked more like a rock star
than many rock stars. What was it with these male musicians
who looked so feminine; the long permed hair, the wearing
of silks and velvets, the wearing of make up; what was that all
about? And they preened and posed like hookers displaying
themselves in a cathouse. Were they trying to get in touch
with their feminine side? Jenny didn't think so, but maybe
in a groupie it was different, a reversing of power relations.

Jackie Brando wore what looked like a stage outfit, all
velvet and shiny, satiny purple with studded leather access-
ories. His red hair was a pre-Raphaelite dream, and his

body was long and willowy. He had a nice smile and nice eyes, and Jenny had been alone and on the road for some time.

Lately she'd found it easier and less complicated to remain celibate when she was on tour, but sometimes difficulty and complication could be attractive too. She noticed Jackie back stage at a gig in a converted skating rink in Stockholm, and again at the post-gig party, and she was definitely interested.

'What do you do?' she asked bluntly.

He flashed her a smile and said (and at least he had the good grace to look embarrassed about it), 'I'm a groupie.'

'A what?' Jenny asked. The party was loud and she thought she must have misheard, but he repeated it and she realized she hadn't.

'Groupie guy, that's me. Use me once, then throw me away like an old set of guitar strings.'

At first she assumed he must be gay. There were enough gay or bi, or at least indiscriminate, male rock musicians around to keep him in business. However, that wasn't what he meant at all.

'I'm a great comfort for the girl bands,' she heard him say. 'I know what it's like for you girls on the road. You get tired. You get so lonely. I know what you want. I can do massage too. I'm clean, I'm healthy, I've got a good suntan and a flat stomach, what more do you want?'

She looked at him with a mixture of amused contempt and disbelief.

'But I'm very discriminating,' he said. 'I'll only sleep with guitarists. Girl drummers, girl keyboard players, girl saxophonists, they leave me absolutely cold. But a woman with

140

a guitar or bass slung across her body gets me hot as an overloaded amplifier valve.

'I don't like to boast, and I wouldn't say I've had them all, but I have references. I have Polaroids. Want to see them?'

Before she could say that wouldn't be necessary he'd whipped out a stack of Polaroids and fanned them out as though they were a pack of cards, and Jenny couldn't help seeing that there were some very famous female faces there, all of them guitar players, many of them undressed, and most of them in advanced stages of sexual arousal.

'Did you buy these somewhere?'

'Now you insult me.'

'Well, I guess you're a good-looking boy but—'

'Looks have got nothing to do with it,' he insisted. 'The reason they sleep with me is because I *respect* them. I tell them all I love the way they play guitar, and it's true. I understand what it's like being an axewoman. I know it's not easy. I'm humble and I'm interested. I may even ask them to show me a few clever chops on the guitar. Like I'd ask you how you produced that incredible vibrato on your last number. And women respect me because they know I respect them. I really couldn't sleep with a female guitarist whose playing I didn't respect.

'I may have been free with my favours, but you know, I've always been true to you in my fashion, Jenny. While ever I was in the hot tub with another I was always thinking about you.'

'Me?' Jenny snorted.

'It's absolutely true. I really adore what you do, Jenny. I love the way you play the guitar. If I needed someone to play guitar in order to save my life, you'd be the one I'd pick. But you don't have to feel the same way about me. You don't have to have any feelings at all. I'm happy for you to use me ruthlessly, then boast about it to your friends. It's all right. I won't think any the less of you for it.'

'Well, that's mighty decent of you, Jackie.'

'Hey, you're not taking me seriously.'

'You noticed.'

'How can I convince you of my good intentions?' he replied.

'I'm not sure that you have good intentions,' Jenny replied.

'That's so untrue, Jenny. I see your long, slender fingers snaking up and down the guitar neck, touching it firmly and precisely, caressing it, coaxing music out of it. I watch you tenderly adjusting the controls. I see your spike-heeled foot slamming down on a stomp box and I want to *be* that guitar. I want to *be* that stomp box.'

Jenny looked at him with amusement.

'You'd better not be all mouth and no trousers,' she said.

Later, in Room 274 of the Stockholm Holiday Inn, Jackie Brando was as good as his word. He was indeed respectful and healthy and relaxing. He knew what she wanted and he provided it, generously and without complaint, and when they lay together afterwards he said, 'Isn't it weird the way people always pull faces when they're playing guitar. You know, before I was a successful male groupie one of the things I always used to wonder was whether the faces people pulled while they were playing guitar were the same as those they pulled when they were having sex.'

'And now you know?' Jenny said.

142

'Yeah, now I know there are a lot of fakers out there. They play their guitar as though they're having some gigantic orgasm, yet when they're actually having a real orgasm their faces look totally different, not nearly so theatrical, not nearly so convincing.

'But you, Jenny, you're no faker; in bed, on stage, hitting the high notes, hitting the orgasm, you're the same. You're real.'

'Gee thanks,' said Jenny ironically, but she was aware that it wasn't the worst compliment she'd ever been paid.

Before the night was over she'd been real another half dozen times.

BEING FRANK

The year is 1954, the setting a hi-fi store in La Mesa, Southern California. There's no air-conditioning in the store, just a floor-standing fan that distractedly stirs up the thick hot air; and just as distractedly, a fourteen-year-old Frank Zappa comes in from the street to look at the cheap R & B singles in the bargain bin.

As he enters the store he passes a great-looking woman who's leaving. Frank's hormones are as unstable as a unicycle and he stops in his tracks to stare. She doesn't look as though she comes from these parts; it's something to do with the way she dresses, really modern, almost futuristic, like maybe she's an air hostess or something else glamorous – well, glamorous for La Mesa. Frank turns his stare into an attempt at a suave, winning smile, like Tony Curtis, or at the very least like Tony Franciosa. Frank's been practising and he thinks he must be getting it nearly right since the woman almost stops, almost makes eye-contact and almost smiles back.

Frank mooches into the centre of the store, flips through the sale records and decides he'll take a couple of Joe Houston platters. He feels in his pocket and counts his change to make sure he has enough money for the purchase.

The cashier eyes him suspiciously. Frank doesn't look like a big spender.

'Who was that woman?' Frank asks as he arrives at the counter.

'I dunno,' the cashier says. 'Some weird foreign dame. English or something. She wanted me to demonstrate one of the record players. She brought in a special record she wanted to hear played. Then after the demo she told me to keep the record.'

'What was the record?' Frank asks.

'I dunno. Some piece a shit.'

'What?'

'It's crazy stuff. Drumming. Stuff like that.'

'I like drum music. I play drums. Put it on again. Lemme hear it.'

The cashier finds Frank strangely persuasive. 'Nah. Well, maybe. Well, OK.' He takes the record and puts it on a turntable, and the needle clicks down on Edgar Varèse's *Ionisation*.

Frank listens and hears what sounds like the start of World War Three. It's jarring and tense, all sharp edges and metallic collisions, but simultaneously there's space and light. It's wild and scary and funny, holy and pagan, all at the same time. It's the stuff of his dreams, the stuff that fills his head, that he lives with every day. Al looks at him and thinks the kid's going to have a seizure or something.

'Actually,' the cashier says, 'the stereo effect ain't bad. Maybe I'll keep it to use as a demonstration record.'

'No,' says Frank. 'I have to have this record. I need it. This is the sound I've been waiting for all my life.'

The cashier thinks of arguing, but why bother? It's too hot, and he suspects the kid's going to get his own way in the end. And what the hell, it's only a record.

'That's all I'm here for, kid,' he says. 'To help complete your education.'

'Yep, that's how I see it,' Frank agrees.

He takes the record and knows he's taken possession of something that's going to be with him for the rest of his life, that's going to be important in defining just what that life is like. He gets home, puts it on the stereo, and from the way his mother and father hate it he knows it's good.

Two days later he's walking home from band practice. His head is full of the marching rhythms he's been practising, but mixed in with them are greasy rock and roll, doo wop and, of course, Varèse. He takes the long way home, goes right to the far edge of town, this town which is all edge and no centre, and just as he's deciding he can't delay his return any longer he sees a car stopped up ahead with the hood raised and someone peering into the engine. He doesn't recognize the car, not even the model, it must be some sort of European job; and then he sees, no, it can't be, he's never been that lucky, there's a woman peering helplessly under the hood. Then he sees she's the one he smiled at in the hi-fi store. This is fantastic. This is fate.

'Car trouble?' he asks.

'Looks like it,' she says.

'I don't know much about cars,' Frank says, 'but I'd be happy to take a look.'

And now she *does* smile at him, the full-strength version,

as though someone's turned on a spotlight and shone it right into Frank's eyes. 'Thanks.' Frank looks under the hood and sees that one of the sparkplug leads is loose. It all seems too easy, too good to be true, but he connects the lead and feels very proud of himself.

'You're brilliant,' she says. 'My name's Jenny Slade, by the way. You're Frank, aren't you?'

'Well yes, but . . .'

'I was just driving around,' says Jenny. 'Need a ride?'

Oh boy. Frank gets in beside her and she sets the car in motion, finds some so-so jazz on the car radio and drives with one hand, looking so good, so sexy, so cool. Frank tries hard to imitate her.

'That was a great record you left behind,' he says.

'I'm glad you liked it. I knew you would.'

'Yeah?'

'What are you planning to do when you grow up, Frank?'

He doesn't like the tone of that question at all. It suggests that she doesn't think he's an equal, that she's the adult and he's just a kid.

'I'd like to be a musician, but I know it's a tough business.'

'You want some advice?' she asks.

Frank is not normally given to listening to advice, especially not from the likes of his dad or his teachers, but this woman isn't quite like them.

'Well, I don't mind hearing it, just so long as I don't have to take it.'

She grins. That's fine. That's her boy.

'First thing,' she says, 'keep the name. Zappa.'

'Yeah? I was wondering about that. You don't think maybe it's too ethnic?'

'No. It's fantastic. It could have been thought up by a committee of marketing men. It's perfect for what you're going to do. You're going to zap things. Second, pretend you're smart.'

'I *am* smart.'

'I know you think you're smart, and maybe you *are* pretty smart for this town. Given the greater shores of smartness, however, you're no rocket scientist.'

'Oh, OK.' Frank sounds confused as though he doesn't know what to do with this bit of advice.

'So stay away from rocket scientists, and away from artists and intellectuals, and away from serious social commentators. Try to spend your life dealing with musicians and rock journalists. By their standards you're a genius.'

He's still not sure whether he's being flattered or insulted.

'And if some idiot college boy comes along and wants to write his Ph.D. about you, pour scorn on the very idea, but don't actually stop him.'

'Doesn't sound so hard.'

'In other words,' Jenny says, 'be cynical.'

'That I can do.'

'Yes, but make sure you're cynical about everything. Not just about parents and police and politicians – everyone's cynical about them. You should be cynical about hippies and rock musicians and the drug culture too.'

'What's a hippie? What's drug culture?'

'It'll become obvious, believe me.'

'Oh, OK.'

148

'What I mean is, be cynical about record companies, but be cynical about record buyers too, even the ones who buy your records. And above all pretend that your music isn't commercial.'

'Yeah? You sure? I mean I'd like to make a lot of money. I'd like the house and the studio up in the Hollywood hills, the cars, the pool, the girls.'

'It's OK, Frank, there are a whole lot of people out there who like music they think is uncommercial. They're your audience. Tell them that by acquiring your records they're being radical and subversive and individualistic and they'll buy your stuff in bulk. Millions of uncommercial units. You can make a fortune by being uncommercial.'

Frank shakes his head. This all sort of makes sense but it'll take some time to sink in.

'But once in a while you may have to stop being totally negative. That's where the guitar playing comes in.'

'Guitar playing?' Frank says. 'But I'm a drummer.'

'You are now, but that's going to have to change.'

'My dad has an old guitar in his closet. I fool around with it sometimes. I guess I could try to play it more seriously if there was going to be some future in it.'

'The future *is* the electric guitar, Frank.'

'If you say so.'

'I do. And that's about it for advice, really.'

'Yeah? It all sounds pretty easy.'

'It may not be as easy as it sounds, but you'll get by. Oh and one more thing, whatever happens, pretend that nobody ever gave you any advice. Pretend you made it all up on your own, pretend that you're entirely your own creation.'

Frank looks rueful. He lights another cigarette, tries to inhale as though he knows what he's doing and says, 'You've been pretty good to me, told me some great stuff. You're smart and attractive, and we seem to get on, so why don't you, you know, complete my education and ball me?'

Jenny looks at him dismissively; suddenly she's light years ahead of him, so genuinely cool, so authentically adult and superior.

'That's another thing you should bear in mind in your music, Frank. Couldn't you try to be a little bit nicer to women?'

Frank raises a thick black eyebrow and says, 'I'm as nice to women as they are to me.'

'Well, maybe I shouldn't press you on this one, since I realize that being vaguely unpleasant about women and sex will probably be a vital part of your career. Sensitive song-writer really isn't going to be your style.'

This much he had worked out for himself but the guitar playing, that's news. He can already see the advantages of being a guitarist rather than a drummer; more chance to show off to the girls, more opportunities to make truly grotesque noise. He sits there for a moment looking out through the windscreen, watching the landscape bend and ripple in the heat.

'Are you for real?' he asks. 'Or are you just a figment of my twisted imagination?'

'You think the two things are mutually exclusive?'

'Well, I don't . . .'

He's confused as all hell. Is it the heat? Is it something in the cigarettes?

'I've been doing far too much talking,' Jenny says. 'After all, you're the guitar genius. I was wondering, is there a piece of advice you'd give to the aspiring guitarist?'

Frank laughs. Until this second he wasn't a guitar genius, not even an aspiring guitarist. Who is he to give advice? Then he thinks, why not? He's regularly confronted by ignorant assholes giving advice on stuff they know nothing about.

'OK,' he says. 'I guess my advice to the aspiring guitar player would be shut up and play your guitar.'

'I like that,' says Jenny. 'I wish I'd said that.'

WILLING FLESH

Bob leans over the bar and says to Kate, 'Rickenbacker, Fender, Gibson, Gretsch, Guild, Steinberger, Kay, Alembic, Harmony, Ibanez, Klein, Kramer, Danelectro, B. C. Rich, Mosrite, Hagstrom, Epiphone, Hamer, Washburn, Vox, Silvertone, Shergold, Watkins, Burns, Patrick Eggle, Paul Reed Smith . . . Are you getting these?'

'I might not remember them all by tomorrow,' Kate admits.

'Well, at least try, because you see these aren't just makers' names, although they *are* makers' names, of course, but they're also a roll of honour. And when you add to these the names of the different models, the Strats and the Teles, the Thunderbirds and the Flying Vs, the Jaguars and the Mustangs, the Pacers, the Bisons, the Presidents, the Meteors, the Sting Rays, the Vikings, the Custom Masqueraders, the Apaches, the Explorers, the Jagstangs, well . . . that's pure twentieth-century poetry.'

'Does it make any difference what guitar you play?' Kate asks.

Bob laughs darkly. 'That's like asking does it matter which cock you suck.'

Oh dear, she thinks, the drink's getting to him. Nevertheless she tries to think through the analogy and even though it seems a needlessly opaque one, with much to be said on both sides, she decides he means yes.

Bob says, 'There's a story, almost certainly apocryphal, of a naive young man who decided he wanted to play the electric guitar. So he went into a guitar shop and bought one. He took it home, strummed it, fiddled with all the knobs but couldn't get any sound out of it. Where was the *sturm und drang* he was looking for? Where was the volume? Where was the skronk? Nowhere, because he didn't realize that you need an amplifier and some speakers before you can get any proper sound out of an electric guitar.

'Instead, in his ignorance, he made the simple observation that his guitar wasn't plugged in yet, that in fact the shop had sold him the guitar without any plug at all. It was now the evening, and too late to go back to the shop and demand the missing plug, so he decided to rig something up for himself. He took a length of electric flex, attached a domestic plug to one end and a jack plug to the other, shoved the jack into the guitar, the plug into the live wall socket and stood helplessly by as his guitar rapidly self-destructed in a shower of sparks and flames.

'That guitar was truly electric, and the chances are it made a pretty unique sound as it died. But that isn't what we normally mean by electric guitar.'

'Hey, I'm not stupid, you know,' Kate protests. 'I've taken on board all the stuff about pickups and magnetic fields.'

He's impressed. 'All right. I didn't mean to insult you. I said before that life is like a guitar solo. But it's also like an electric guitar itself. That's because it's expensive, not

153

necessarily all that pretty, surprisingly fragile and all too likely to go out of tune. It's also far too easy to fetishize and get over-attached to, and then some bastard is only too likely to take it away from you. You know what I mean?'

'I think so.'

'Some people give their guitars names. They call them "Lucille" and silliness like that.'

'Always women's names?'

'Not always, no.'

'I'm glad. That was quite some guitar Jenny Slade was playing tonight. Even I could tell that.'

'Yes, it's special. I can tell you the date and place where she first used it if you like.'

'No thanks.'

He's a little disappointed not to be able to further demonstrate his expertise but he lets it go.

'Like most guitarists,' he says, 'Jenny tried a lot of different guitars before she found the one that suited her.'

'Does Jenny Slade have a name for her guitar?'

Bob looks at her mysteriously. It's a banal question, yet it's more telling than she realizes.

'If it had a name,' he says, 'it would be called "Greg". "Greg Wintergreen".'

'What kind of name is that?'

He reaches into one of his bags and comes up with another copy of the *Journal of Sladean Studies*.

'This will explain everything.'

'More post-modernism?'

'Post-modern and almost certainly apocryphal.'

'I can hardly wait.'

GUITARMORPHOSIS

Greg Wintergreen woke from uneasy dreams one morning to find himself changed into an electric guitar. He was lying on his back, which was of a lacquered hardness, and when he lifted his headstock a little he became aware of his belly with scratch plate and tremolo arm. His strings, of a pitifully light gauge, vibrated ineffectually.

What's going on? he thought.

This was no dream. His room, a normal human room except perhaps a little too small to allow him to play electric guitar at the volume he would have liked, lay peacefully between the four familiar walls. Above the table, which was littered with guitar tutors, CDs and guitar magazines, hung the picture he had recently cut out of a magazine and stuck to the wall. It showed Bonnie Raitt cradling her trademark blue Stratocaster.

Greg's attention shifted to the window. Raindrops hit the glass in a loose four-four beat, and he felt as though he finally knew what the blues were all about. Why don't I go back to sleep and maybe I'll dream about turning into Stevie Ray Vaughan instead, he thought, but somehow he knew this was going to be impossible.

He heard the voices of his mother, father and sister outside the door of his room, all urging him to get up.

'Greg, you'll be late for work. Again,' his mother shouted. He tried to reply and gave a start when he heard the sound of his own voice; unmistakably his, but blended with it was the sound of a humbucking pickup. Fortunately he was plugged in to a small practice amp. 'I'll be right down,' he said musically.

The strangeness of his voice went unnoticed. Perhaps his family thought he was having an early-morning guitar practice. Such things were not unknown.

In truth he did want to get up, get dressed, go downstairs, and he thought that when he'd done those things he might be able to consider his plight more rationally. But having no arms or legs he could see that these simple tasks were likely to prove impossible. He stayed where he was, silent and immobile, and glad that he'd locked his bedroom door before going to sleep the previous night.

He lay there a long time and heard various comings and goings in the house, and then his sister came to the door and informed him in a whisper, 'The shop manager's here.' Greg worked in a music shop and his manager had agreed to stop by and give him a lift into work this morning since it was stocktaking day and they needed an early start.

'Greg, it's Frank here,' the manager shouted cheerily through the door. 'Is this a wind-up or what? I know the tills have been short lately, but I never thought you was the culprit. And then there was that bit of bother over the echo unit you took in a part-exchange deal; all right, so it was nicked, but I still thought you was an honest lad. However, now I find you're taking the piss and you're making me have second thoughts.'

Greg tried to speak and this time it appeared they could no longer understand him. All they could hear was the sound of a guitar.

'This is no time to be practising your scales!' Greg's father yelled, and he yanked the door handle as hard as he could and succeeded in breaking the flimsy lock.

Father, mother, sister and music-shop manager entered the bedroom.

'All right, I'll get up, I'll come to work, if someone can only give me a hand,' Greg said plaintively.

But again nobody understood him. They gathered round and stared down at the electric guitar lying there on the duvet, and they were terrified and speechless. True, a guitar lying on a bed was not in itself terrifying, but as they looked at its frets, its machine heads, at the grain of the body, at the general patina of the thing, there could be no doubt that this musical instrument before them was their own Greg Wintergreen.

The shop manager fled the house, saying he mustn't be late for stocktaking, and Greg's father too said he had an important meeting that he couldn't afford to miss. Even Greg's mother and sister slipped from the room, closing the door hurriedly and firmly behind them. Greg fell into a feverish sleep.

Not until dusk did he wake again. The room had been tidied and was warm, and someone had left a tray of food for him. It was a thoughtful gesture but a futile one. Even if he'd been hungry, which he was not, by what possible means could he have consumed the food?

More helpfully, he was aware that someone had tuned his strings but he had been unplugged from the practice amp. He hummed to himself thinly and very quietly in a lochrian mode, but not for too long. He didn't want to disturb his family any further. All evening he could hear their voices downstairs and he didn't doubt that they were talking about him, but they went to bed without coming in to bid him goodnight.

Next morning his sister returned to the bedroom, took away the untouched tray and came back with guitar polish and a cloth and began to buff the surface of Greg's body. His father and mother refused to come near, although he did overhear a conversation in which his father referred to his son as a layabout and said that things were going to be considerably harder for the family without Greg's wage coming in. They seemed already resigned to the fact that Greg's transformation was permanent. It took Greg much longer to accept that.

As the days passed, his sister continued to administer to him but there was a growing reluctance about it and he soon realized that she found the sight of him unbearable, as though she were looking at a corpse or a mummy. Not long after that she arrived carrying a guitar case and placed Greg inside it to spare herself the torment of having to look at him.

His mother and father came at last to see their transformed son. It was traumatic for both of them, and perhaps specially so for his father, who in a fit of grief-stricken rage picked Greg up and yanked at his strings until he'd broken three of them. One of the strings snapped at him, whipped the back of his hand and left him with a long, red cut. It took Greg's sister a lot of effort to dissuade their father from chopping Greg up there and then for firewood.

What point was there in tuning a guitar with only three strings? What point in polishing it? What point in even opening the case?

Greg's sister began to neglect him. She did not come to clean his room and it soon began to gather dust, and for a time it became a depository for old boxes and pieces of furniture not wanted in the rest of the house.

But then Greg's mother decided that since Greg was no longer making much use of his room she might as well rent it out. The lodger she found was a bearded, duffle-coat-wearing saxophonist, leader of a jazz trio. Like many jazz players he was rather dismissive of the electric guitar and certainly didn't want one cluttering up his room. So Greg was moved into the living room, where for a brief time he lived behind the television set, propped up against the hostess trolley, but when Greg's father developed the theory that the guitar's presence was affecting television reception, Greg was moved again, taken out of the body of the house and condemned to a damp corner of the utility room.

Greg was now apparently well out of the way, and yet he was still a grim reminder to the family of their own dysfunctional state.

'It has to go,' Greg's sister said, with resolve. 'It's the only way. We must try to stop thinking of it as Greg. The Greg we know is gone forever. I'll take it to some second-hand music shops and try to sell it.'

She began at the store where Greg himself had worked, but Frank, the manager, took one look at the guitar and said he didn't want that thing in his shop. And so it went at other music shops. Although the buyers couldn't quite put their finger on what was wrong with the guitar, or why they wouldn't take it off her hands, they all made it clear they wanted nothing to do with the instrument.

In despair Greg's sister explained her plight to the family's lodger. Was there perhaps someone in his circle of musicians who could find a use for an old but little-used electric guitar? He was not optimistic but came back later and said there was a band called the Flesh Guitars who could probably make use of Greg, although of course he had not mentioned to them the guitar's anthropomorphic nature. A deal was agreed.

It was at a time in musical history when Jenny Slade and the Flesh Guitars were in their most nihilistic, confrontational phase. It was a period when they were getting through guitars at a frightening rate, smearing them with pig's intestines, attacking them with strimmers, electric sanders, caulking irons, beating them against walls, floors, ceiling, and finally smashing them to pieces against the speaker cabinets of the PA. The semi-naked bass player might then rub her crotch with fragments of the guitar neck in a mood of Dionysian abandon.

It was not what any self-respecting family would have wanted for their son. Fortunately Jenny Slade knew a good instrument when she saw one. She played a couple of chords on it and saw at once that it was too good to abuse and destroy. She wanted that guitar, and wild horses wouldn't have taken it from her. Naturally, Jenny would have been a great guitarist whatever guitar she used, but there was something about the Greg Wintergreen guitar that was perfectly suited to her technique. It became her main instrument, and she never looked back.

Reprinted from the *Journal of Sladean Studies*
Volume 8 Issue 3

TWINS

Perhaps after the fiasco of their 'tour' and the Psychology Club gig Jenny Slade should have stayed well clear of Tom Scorn, and no doubt she would have if he hadn't kept coming up with such weird and exciting music. She had watched with fascination as he changed from a young, naive upstart into a major player in the world of experimental music. He met up with Jenny again while waiting for a plane to fly to the Greenland Thrash Elevator Festival, where they were both making guest appearances.

Dispensing with pleasantries he slid a tape into a DAT player and asked Jenny to listen. She had never heard anything quite like the noises that came out. There was lots of space and silence, great pools of inky stillness in which there was little or no music, but then there would be an explosion of percussion or a streak of dissonant piano chords followed by more silence. Next there would be a thud of bass guitar noise, again brief stabs and attacks of sound, music wrestled out of the very craw of the instrument, followed perhaps by the thin rasp of a high hat, then silence again.

'Check out that extended technique,' Scorn blurted, 'that non-canonical praxis.'

He was right. Jenny could hear that conventional technique had been discarded. Notions of good playing had been sent packing, and yet there was something compelling in the music. For all that the music rejected the easy pleasures, it drew you in and was surprisingly easy to listen to.

'It's something special,' Jenny said. 'Who is it?'

'The Hormone Twins,' Scorn said. 'They're real twins.'

'And is that their real name?'

'Sure. Bobby and Walter Hormone. I think maybe it's French.'

'Are they new?'

'Very. I was hoping you'd play on their début album. I'm producing it. I thought your presence would give them a bit of stature, and help you keep in touch with the younger audience.'

'I'm in touch with all sorts of audiences,' Jenny assured him.

'But you'll do it, yes?'

'OK.'

'Promise you won't change your mind?'

'Why would I do that?'

'Because Walter and Bobby are only eight years old.'

'Jesus.'

'You promised.'

'OK, I promised.'

Jenny believed in keeping her promises.

The recording studio, in a converted garden centre in Telford, was retro to the point of antiquity. The microphone stands were rusty, the baffle boards were marked with many generations of muso graffiti, the control room was inside a greenhouse that had once been used for growing orchids.

Jenny's own equipment was set up neatly in a corner, while that belonging to the Hormone Twins was laid out haphazardly all over the rest of the studio. There was a drum kit, tubular bells, a glockenspiel, a piano, Hammond organ, some cheesy early synthesizers, an array of trumpets and flutes, a siren, a vast Chinese gong, plus huge baskets full of miniature percussion instruments, penny whistles, Jews harps and kazoos. The place looked like a musical play-room.

There was no sign of the twins but Jenny could hear boys' voices coming from outside the studio, from the area where the fruit trees and garden statuary had once been kept. The trees were now blackened and denuded and the statuary was in ruins but the twins were finding it a great place to play. They were grunting and screaming and throwing stones and chunks of broken statue at each other.

Jenny was no great lover of children, and these were less lovable than most. There was something stunted and porcine about them, something lumpen yet violent. Scorn rounded them up and dragged them into the studio. Once indoors their exuberance disappeared and they stood awkwardly saying nothing and sniggering like imbeciles. Jenny said hello and the twins' replies were inaudible.

Scorn shrugged. 'Hey, they're kids. They're musicians. They speak through their music.' And with that he went into the booth.

The twins were wearing an approximation of school uniform, but from a very weird school. They wore short

163

trousers, very Angus Young, blazers and school caps; but the uniforms were made of some weird metallic material and edged with hide. The boys wore motorcycle boots, five or six sizes too large, and instead of school ties they had nooses hanging round their necks.

'So what would you like me to play?' Jenny asked.

She hadn't been foolish enough to believe that there'd be songs, or even loose compositions, but she was hoping for some sort of guidance. All Scorn said was, 'Start playing and we'll see what happens.' That was OK with Jenny too. She made sure her guitar was in tune, strapped it around her and waited for the twins to take up position with one of the instruments, but they showed no sign of doing that, just stood at the centre of the studio muttering aggressively at each other. What the hell? Scorn displayed no concern and let the tape run. So Jenny began improvising some tricky chord progressions and hoped the kids would eventually join in.

They didn't. They continued to mutter and although their words never became audible, the boys became much more animated. The conversation was turning into a loud, fierce argument, which in turn became physical. They started to push each other, shoulder to shoulder, and when push came to shove, one of them, Jenny had no idea which since she couldn't tell them apart, was sent reeling backwards so that he fell on to the drum kit.

Jenny was about to stop playing and help the kid up, but Scorn was gesturing at her from the control room, telling her to keep playing, to act as though nothing was wrong. It was easier said than done but Jenny continued the improvisation she'd started as the boys continued to fight, their fury increasing into an all-out flurry of flying fists and motorcycle boots. At first Jenny had the feeling she was providing the soundtrack for a violent, silent, slapstick comedy, however the twins were anything but silent. They squealed and yelled, and once in a while one of them crashed into the stand holding the tubular bells or had his head banged against the keyboard of the Hammond organ.

It only gradually dawned on Jenny that these violent noises and occasional rhythmical outbursts were strangely familiar. Although they didn't reproduce exactly the music from the demo tape, the sounds were precisely similar in kind. She saw that this was the 'extended technique' Scorn had spoken of, a method of beating each other up with a quasi-musical racket produced as a side effect.

She felt like a childminder who'd abandoned her charges, fiddling while Rome burned, a boxing referee who was allowing a free-for-all. Surely adults had some obligation to prevent children damaging themselves, even if it was for the sake of art. Yet Scorn showed no signs of stepping in, and to be fair, the twins seemed to be having the time of their lives.

Unsure exactly what kind of guitar noise best suited these circumstances Jenny cranked up her echo unit and made a lot of spacy noise. The twins took no notice, but Scorn smiled approvingly.

Jenny could not see how or when this session would end; whether the twins would stop because of boredom or exhaustion, or whether they'd carry on until one or other was bludgeoned into unconsciousness. After half an hour one of them had a nose bleed, and after forty-five minutes or so one of them hoisted up the other, using the rope around his neck, and shoved his head into the innards of the grand piano ('Very John Cage,' cooed Scorn) before running from the studio.

Even Jenny had to admit that the piano strings made a lovely raw, loose, opulent sound, but the boy remained quite motionless. She pulled him from the guts of the instrument and sat him on the piano stool. Still stunned, and quite oblivious to Jenny's presence, Walter turned round, addressed the keyboard and began a long improvisation, all diminished sevenths and suspended fourths. It was rather wonderful and when she joined in, Jenny was stretched to keep up. She was keen to hear the playback but to her dismay she learned that Scorn hadn't bothered to record this part of the proceedings. He said it was tame and old hat. All he wanted were the bangs and crashes and scrapes. And just one hour into the session he announced that it was over. He'd have to do a bit of serious remixing, maybe add a few musical touches of his own, but he had enough material for an album.

He appeared to be right. *Siam: The Hormone Twins Play The Music Of Tom Scorn* was rush released and in the shops a month or so later. Reviews were mixed. Jenny Slade, credited only as a session player, was always singled out by the critics. Some said she was the glue holding the whole thing together. Others said she sounded constrained and inhibited compared to the 'free-spirited playing' of the twins. Jenny was just about able to laugh it off. What did critics know? What difference did their opinion make? She was sort of glad she'd worked with the twins. It had been an experience, if not a very edifying one.

She never played with them again but she watched their careers with interest. Being a prodigy is a difficult and dangerous business. For one thing, prodigies grow up and have to prove themselves all over again. For the Hormone Twins there was another danger. As small boys they'd lacked the ability to do each other much physical damage. As they became adolescents they developed bulk and strength, and their fights became much more violent. Cuts, abrasions, black eyes became commonplace, an essential part of their act, and it seemed only a matter of time before one of them seriously injured the other.

The moment of crisis came when Bobby slammed the body of a double-bass down on Walter's right hand and broke two of his fingers. In one way it might appear not to matter. The twins could 'play' just as well with broken hands as without. They could play with broken arms, legs, skulls, as far as that went. But this injury was a watershed. After Walter's fingers had healed he announced he was now a pacifist and wasn't going to fight with Bobby any more, wasn't even going to defend himself against his attacks.

The first gig after Walter's return was a wild one. Bobby tore into his brother, kicking and punching him for all he was worth. But when Walter stood silent and inert, just getting hit and soaking up the punishment, Bobby soon tired of the procedure. After all, Bobby was a boy who liked to fight, not an outright sadist. He wanted an opponent not a human punchbag. He stopped hitting his brother and the gig ended prematurely in silent confusion.

Jenny was called in, not to pour oil on troubled waters, but rather the reverse, to see if she couldn't stir up a bit of the old sibling rivalry. She talked to them, suggested they might wear protective clothing or use some safer martial arts techniques, but it was useless. Walter said he was going to pursue a career as a solo pianist; a bit of Liberace and a lot of Thelonius Monk. Jenny didn't try to argue with him. She still thought his piano playing was pretty good.

Bobby was left with a far greater dilemma. He wanted to remain a Hormone Twin and play the way he always had, and for a while he did. He would arrive in the studio or on stage and proceed to throw himself around as though he were being beaten up by a squad of invisible men. He'd launch himself over the drums or the vibraphone, slam the piano lid down on his own hand, hit himself over the head with a saxophone. It was heart-felt but somehow it never quite worked. It seemed too forced, too premeditated. It wasn't the same without Walter.

Both of the boys individually asked Jenny to play with them, but she declined. It seemed to her that the moment and the magic had gone. Things got worse for the twins. Walter found himself playing cocktail piano in a Chinese restaurant in Carlisle, where 'Chopsticks' was requested a dozen times a night, and Bobby became a comedy mime act. Audiences spurned them both. Tom Scorn now described them as 'shallow and revisionist' and said he regretted having produced their first record. Before long they disappeared completely and the more macabre fans talked of fights to the death and bizarre suicide pacts.

Jenny didn't know what she believed, wasn't really sure

whether the boys were alive or dead. She hoped the former, although she could see why they might have chosen the latter. However, regardless of their actual fates, from then on whenever Jenny was in the studio and a cymbal toppled over or a microphone fell off its stand, apparently for no reason, she'd cross herself and say, 'There go the ghosts of poor Walter and Bobby.'

BEAUTY TIPS WITH JENNY SLADE:

Number two: the boobs

Jenny Slade says, 'You know, if there's one thing I get asked more than any other, it's this: "Jenny," girls will say, "is my chest too heavily built for me ever to become a truly good guitarist?"

'I always try to be sympathetic. But first I say, is it really that big a problem? Unless you're colossally stacked there are probably ways of getting round it.

'Let's face it, lots of guys who have massive beer bellies are still able to play guitar, and the truth is, most beer bellies are bigger than most breasts.

'But if you genuinely find it a problem, if you're really built like a pre-op Amazon, and if you're really serious about the guitar, then a breast reduction operation has got to be worth considering. Either that or you're going to have to change to playing pedal steel.'

Reprinted from the *Journal of Sladean Studies*
Volume 4 Issue 1

NUDE GUITAR GIRLS

In the Havoc Bar and Grill Kate and Bob have settled down to a boozy quietness. There's lots more Kate wants to know about Jenny Slade, and she has no doubt that Bob has oceans more to tell, but for a while it's enough to keep all that stuff on hold, to savour the whisky, to savour the night.

This quietness lasts no time at all, as the sleeping drunk on the other side of the bar wakes up, is reborn into flustered, disorientated life. He gets to his feet, jinks across to the jukebox and shovels some coins into the slot. Kate knows there's no Jenny Slade on the machine and there's no other music she could bear to listen to right now, so she flips the switch behind the bar that turns it off. The drunk is thrown into lumbering confusion. Unable to understand what's happened to his selection, he approaches the bar and orders another drink.

'I heard you talking about girls and guitars,' he says. 'And they just happen to be two of my special interests. Here's to 'em.'

He drinks a toast in honour of girls and guitars.

'Here's to all those nude guitar girls,' he says. 'You know who they are, though you don't necessarily know their names. They appear in ads. They appear on album covers, on posters, in magazines. They appear on bedroom walls. They get their images stuck on guitar cases, on the insides of lockers, in the windows of guitar shops; you know the type.

'Sometimes they're hugging the guitar as though it's a mighty phallus, or at least a phallic substitute; not as a dildo exactly, since the guitar has too many hard, sharp edges for most tastes, and God knows it's a little large for most anatomical configurations, but you get the point, nevertheless. Here's to 'em.'

He drinks again.

'Hey, am I drinking alone here?' he demands of Kate and Bob. 'Next time I propose a toast I want you both to join in.'

Kate eyes him suspiciously, just another sucker, but she knows that talk of women and 'girls' can lead to bad, unpredictable behaviour in the Havoc clientele.

The drunk continues, 'Here's to the nude guitar girl who's an adornment for the guitar player. He stands fondling the guitar while she stands fondling him. She's impressed, thrilled, attracted to and turned on by his chunky yet stream-lined axe. She admires his poise, his dexterity, his ability to wield that huge thing with authority yet delicacy. If she's wearing clothes at all they'll be skimpy and few and they'll soon be shed.

'Or maybe she'll be stretched out atop a stack of amplifiers and speaker cabinets, with tousled hair, a "come and get it" expression in her eyes that the manufacturer hopes the punter will confuse with lust and transfer from the girl to the hardware.

172

'Here's to all those naked girls on the original *Electric Ladyland* cover, to the barely pubescent teeny holding the silver aeroplane on the Blind Faith album. Here's to all the babes on all the Ohio Players albums. Here's to the girl pleasuring herself with a Tokai copy of a Stratocaster in guitar magazine ads, the legend "Tokai is Coming" printed behind her back.

'I've seen 'em all, bare bodies coiled with guitar strings and guitar leads, naked women posing in front of banks of speakers, plectrums displayed in deep cleavages. I've seen pickups strategically placed on nipples to retain some crass notion of decency, if not dignity. I've seen taut, sweaty bodies creating an objective correlative for the virtues of pedals and stomp boxes. Here's to 'em.'

With a certain reluctance, though with a considerable urge to placate, Kate and Bob drink. Bob knows that Kate is being made uncomfortable by the drunk, and he can see her point all too clearly, though on a different night, in a different bar, he knows he might be proposing similar toasts himself.

The drunk says, 'Here's to the girls who got their tits out for the lads, who got their tits out so the audience would have something to entertain them while the lead guitarists went into long, laboured solos. Here's to Stacia of Hawkwind, and Wendy O. Williams of the Plasmatics, and sometimes Grace Slick, and sometimes even Siouxsie Sioux, and certainly P. J. Harvey and definitely Patti Smith.

'Exploited? Oh come now, surely that's just the name of a band. Here's to 'em.'

This time Kate doesn't pick up her drink, won't humour

the drunk at all, and Bob decides his place is right with her.

'No, we can't drink to that, I'm afraid,' he says.

For a second the drunk looks dangerously agitated. Who are these people that think they're too good to drink with him? Maybe he should take one of them outside, probably the guy, though not necessarily, and see what he's made of. Then the booze and tiredness roll in again and he simply can't be bothered.

'OK,' he says, 'so *you* propose a toast.'

After due consideration Bob Arnold says, 'Here's to the *ironic* nude guitar girls. Here's to the Slits all wet mud and atavism. Here's to post-feminist nudity, to the vocalist in Tribe 8 who sings topless wearing a strap-on. Here's to Courtney Love letting it all flop out, having her doll parts mauled by sticky fingers from the moshing pit.

'And here's, especially, to poor, poor Laurel Fishman, who is remembered, if at all, for having been vaginally penetrated by Steve Vai with his guitar head. The episode is recorded in a particularly nasty song by Frank Zappa. Here's to you, Laurel. Here's to all you girls. You're the genuine article no doubt, the real thing, the live wire. Mind how you go. Forgive us for being young and callow, for being in love with the guitar. It was so much easier than being in love with real women.'

'OK, I'll drink to that,' says the drunk, and all three of them raise their whiskies.

The drunk's glass is now empty and he seems glad of it. Bob's attempt at a toast was just one more baffling element in this long and befuddled night.

'Here's to Jenny Slade,' the drunk says thickly, and he

waves his empty glass in the air before returning to his table to resume his alcoholic slumbers.

'Thanks for the solidarity there, Bob,' Kate says.

'It's not a problem,' says Bob.

'I've got nothing against nude guitar girls, you understand,' she says confessionally, 'just against unpredictable drunks.'

'Oh well, in that case,' and Bob produces another issue of the *Journal of Sladean Studies* from one of his bags.

PERFORMANCE NOTES – SHIMMERS

Bob Arnold recalls an especially challenging Jenny Slade gig

Lately Jenny Slade has been denying that she ever made a habit of appearing nude on stage; but anyone who ever saw the Flesh Guitars play the composition 'Shimmers' (described as 'a performance piece for more intimate spaces') would surely beg to differ.

The Flesh Guitars were operating as a drummerless six-piece at the time, two men, four women, all of them guitarists. The players were prodigiously gifted unknowns who regarded Jenny Slade with a certain awe, and would willingly have followed her into the darkest regions of guitar hell.

The stage was set with a dozen guitars, a few on floor stands, others suspended on racks at waist level; some were bass guitars, some twelve strings; some were hooked up to multiple effects units. Illumination was kept enticingly low, a swathe of purple light bleeding into shades of coral. The six band members took to the stage, some of them a little tentatively, some with a defiant confidence.

It would take the audience little or no time to realize that all six band members were naked; Jenny Slade included. Her later claims that she wore a flesh-coloured body-stocking simply won't wash. Even the most blasé crowds would be captivated by six nude guitarists. Was it just a cheap gimmick? No. Genuine Jenny Slade fans knew better than that, but even they could have had little idea of what was to come.

As the audience peered more closely at the musicians, as their eyes got used to the dim light, they would see amid the dappling of line and shadow that there was something unusual, something *extra* about the nudity. It could take a long time to work out precisely what was going on, but sooner or later one would realize that each guitarist's body was spiked in dozens of places by acupuncture needles, all of which had been left *in situ*, their points lodged in the guitarists' flesh.

They moved towards their instruments and positioned themselves before them. They stood an inch or two away. Then, as their bodies moved, acupuncture needles would sway and make metallic contact with the guitar strings. Sometimes several needles would touch different strings or different parts of the strings simultaneously. There would be glistening ripples, glissandos and arpeggios. The sounds produced might be clean and resonant one moment, the next they might be just random scrapes.

The sonic possibilities for six people of different builds and body types performing movements that ranged from the barely perceptible to the downright violent, touching the strings glancingly or furiously as the case might be, with each guitar displaying its own distinctive, musical signature, were all but limitless. Performances could go on for two hours or more, until the performers were physically or creatively exhausted. The piece was so demanding that it remained in the Flesh Guitars' repertoire for less than six months.

Only one, rather inadequate bootleg recording exists of 'Shimmers'. It is not much prized by collectors, whereas a pirate video of a performance at a private party in a converted corned beef factory in Rio de Janeiro has been known to change hands for staggeringly high prices. Jenny Slade, despite her denials, has never looked better.

Reprinted from the *Journal of Sladean Studies*
Volume 7 Issue 4

A HARD DAY IN THE LIFE

'Guess who invented the plectrum?'

The question was fired at Jenny Slade by a famous Hollywood movie producer, Howie Howardson by name, a member of the new Hollywood, the *very* new Hollywood. He appeared to her as a series of slurred fashion statements: cowboy boots, a soul patch, an orange crew-cut, a turquoise ring as big as a gull's egg, a waistcoat made of giant fish scales, sunglasses in the shape of ultra-wide cinema screens.

'No idea,' Jenny replied.

'Go on, guess,' Howardson said with boyish enthusiasm.

'Will Scarlet,' she offered fatuously.

'No, not even warm,' Howardson replied. 'It was Sappho. Goddamn Sappho invented the plectrum. How about that?'

'I didn't know that,' Jenny admitted.

'But you've heard of Sappho. Am I right?'

'Yes.'

'So I don't have to tell you she was this major Greek, lyre-playing lipstick lezzie. She plucked the strings, she pulled the babes. There's a vase painting or some damn thing that proves she was the first-ever plectrum user.'

'That's incredible,' Jenny said, trying to show a willingness to be impressed.

'I'm just telling you this information so you'll have some idea of the depth of research that's gone into this project.'

Ah yes, the project. Jenny knew she must have been flown here for a reason, even if that reason had yet to be revealed. The office was in a converted fall-out shelter, a long, low-ceilinged tunnel with white concrete walls. Here Howardson displayed his love of art and electricity; the walls were hung with early Paolozzis, Gwen Johns, late Rosenquists, a couple of Frank Stellas, some important Braques. And these canvases were interspersed with and lit by neon shop signs, illuminated petrol pumps, barber's poles, lamps in the shapes of fish, dragons, Swiss chalets, chandeliers hung low with bunches of mutated grapes and ping-pong balls. It hurt the eyes to look at it all. Perhaps that was why Howardson wore such impenetrable shades.

'Maybe I'm getting ahead of myself,' he said. 'First thing I ought to say is that we love your work. We're passionate about it. I especially loved your music video, the one where you've got the big supermarket set and it looks as though it's being filmed by a security camera. It has a fabulous retro look. And there's no posing, none of that lousy over-acting you get in so many videos.'

Jenny quietly said, 'Thank you,' and tactfully didn't point out to him that it was no 'set' at all but a real supermarket and that the retro security camera look was achieved by using an actual modern security camera, and the lack of posing was because you don't need to pose very much when

180

you're doing your shopping. Still, what did it matter so long as he liked it, so long as he *said* he liked it?

'You remember when you were at school?' Howardson asked, getting down to business now. 'I guess it's the same in England, how they'd get you to write the life story of a penny and you'd have to track it from being pressed, going in and out of the bank, through all the pockets and purses of the people who owned it, through slot machines and one-armed bandits till it finally fell into a drain. Or maybe you remember those portmanteau movies like *The Yellow Rolls-Royce* where the film tells the story of everyone who had the car. Well, we want to do the same with a plectrum.'

Jenny struggled to keep her composure in the face of this absurdity. She attempted to remain alert and interested-looking but she feared she might be failing.

'First scene shows Sappho playing her axe,' said Howardson, 'which is actually some sort of harp, but that could be changed. So she has a few adventures but eventually she dies, and the plectrum goes missing for a thousand years or so, and then suddenly Henry the Eighth is using it at Hampton Court to play "Greensleeves" on a lute. Centuries later it turns up in Chicago being used by Muddy Waters, then before long it finds its way to Vegas where it's used by Elvis. He hands it to someone in the audience who gives it to Johnny Thunders who's so stoned he drops it and only years later is it rediscovered by Joe Satriani, or maybe Sheryl Crow, or whoever's hottest when we finally cast this thing.

'So you see, the possibilities are literally endless. Great moments in plectrum history, past, present and future. There'll be a script real soon. Yeah, and we're also really keen to have a sci-fi element set in the future. Maybe some twenty-first-century teenager finds the plectrum, but the electric guitar has died out by then and he doesn't know what it is, so he goes to the local museum, steals an old Gibson, and the rest you can guess. So what do you say, Jenny, are you interested?'

'Yes,' she said with all the feigned enthusiasm she could muster. She knew this was no time for reservations; she could have those later. 'You mean you want me to compose the music for the film?'

Howardson moved uneasily in his chair, twirled his rings around his fingers a couple of times. At last he said, 'Well, that's a possibility, Jenny, although I have to admit it wasn't a possibility we'd actually thought of. We had someone else kind of pencilled in for that job. More what we had in mind was for you to be the film's plectrum consultant.'

Jenny gawped.

He continued, 'You see, a lot of big-name actors and actresses are crying out to be in this movie, and most of them have scarcely even *seen* a plectrum before. They sure as hell won't know how to hold one. That's where you come in; to make their plectrum use look authentic. Don't worry, we're gonna get somebody else to deal with the fretting hand.'

Jenny leaned back, stared fixedly at a lamp in the shape of a bison and said nothing. She was aware that for the first time she actually had Howardson's attention.

'I could pick up that bison lamp,' she said, 'and I could run it along my guitar neck, pull it across the strings and, hey presto, suddenly it would be a plectrum.'

'I see,' Howardson said, utterly uncomprehending but still upbeat.

'A plectrum is what a plectrum does,' Jenny went on. 'Thurston Moore shoves a drum stick into his strings and turns the drum stick into a plectrum. Tom Verlaine saws at his strings with a metal file. Reeves Gabrels coaxes noise out of his guitar using a vibrator.

'Whether it's a piece of plastic, a length of steel pipe, or an electric angle-grinder they're all conceptually and functionally performing the role of the plectrum. When some poodle-head guitarist rubs his guitar with his crotch, he's saying that even the mighty phallus can be reduced to the status of a plectrum. Sappho might have had a lot to say about that.'

Howardson grinned wickedly. 'I love a plectrum coach who talks dirty,' he said.

Some time later . . .

'I'm worried about my hands, Jenny.'

The speaker was Megan Floss, the actress who would be playing the part of Patti Smith in the movie. Megan was thirty-three years old. She used to have a reputation for being a real hard body, but in her last couple of movies she'd looked fat and puffy. She'd had jowls for Chrissake! So she'd been working hard, getting toned up and thinned down, getting tanned and tucked. Everybody told her she'd never looked better, but they *would* say that, wouldn't they? She wanted to believe it. She knew her butt looked good, she knew her tits looked good, and so they should; they were straight out of the catalogue. She knew her face would look

183

OK, she'd trust this lighting cameraman with more than her life. Everyone told her everything was going to be fine, but that still left her with a truckload of insecurities and they had to come out somewhere.

'There's no need to worry,' Jenny said. 'That's why I'm here.'

'But I'm worried about the things you can't fix, things like poor skin tone, wrinkles, damaged cuticles.'

Yep, Megan was focusing all her stress, all her anxiety on this one area, her plectrum hand.

'It'll be fine, really,' Jenny said.

She showed Megan how to hold a plectrum and after five or six hours the actress seemed to be getting the hang of it. She sent for an assistant, who entered holding a mirror for her to observe her hand in. She looked. She shrieked; a high-pitched, attention-seeking, filmic shriek.

'Oh my God, I'm going to have to wear gloves!'

'Well, I'm not the director,' Jenny said, 'but I can't see anybody playing guitar in gloves.'

'Then what's the alternative?'

'We could always use a hand model.'

'A hand model!' Megan bawled. 'What do you think I am? I'm a serious actress. I have integrity. I have a reputation to think of. I'd rather die than use a stand-in. Right, now we understand each other, let's get down to some serious plectrum practice.'

Later that same week . . .

'Now about this plectrum thing . . .'

'Yes?' said Jenny.

She was talking to Michael Cutlass, a movie star of the old school; craggy, iron-chested, toupeed. He was being cast against type in the role of Jimmy Page.

'I'm going to need a lot of help from you on this one,' Cutlass said.

'That's what I'm here for,' Jenny replied.

'Because I want to get it right. And more than that, I want the plectrum technique to be part of the characterization. I want the audience to be able to look at the way I hold the plectrum and say, there goes a real man, a strong man, tough but not insensitive, a man's man but also a woman's man, the kind of guy who can ride a horse, use a gun, fly a Lear jet, make love to a couple of women, all with consummate ease. I want the way I hold that plectrum to say that I'm a poet, a fighter, a man of integrity, a man who's known pain, who'd be a good father, a good son, the kind of guy who'd lend you his last fifty bucks, the kind of guy who could wrestle naked with his buddies and yet there'd be no hint of queerness. You know what I'm saying?'

'I'll see what I can do, Mr Cutlass.'

'In fact,' he continued, 'I've been thinking maybe there's something effete about using a plectrum at all. I think maybe I'm more the kind of guy who wouldn't fiddle around with some cheesy little bit of plastic, but more the sort of guy who'd use his bare hands, feel the wood and steel on fingers, wrench melodies with his own skin and bone. You got me?'

'Oh yes, I've got you all right,' Jenny said.

And later still.

'This is boring.'

185

'Not only for you,' Jenny said.

Jenny was now giving tuition to eleven-year-old Trixie Picasso, who was appearing in a fantasy sequence about the childhood of Joan Jett. The kid was a monster: cute-looking, big-eyed, a sweet smile, huge bubbles of blonde hair and the disposition of a cornered rat. She also, incidentally, bore not the slightest resemblance to Joan Jett, whether old or young.

'Guitars are boring,' she said. 'They're old hat. I mean, who needs 'em. Gimme a sampler and a sequencer and a drum machine and you're history, lady.'

'You think so, huh?'

'I know so.'

'And why do you think that?' Jenny said sweetly, humouring the brat.

'Well, the main thing is that time is no longer a meaningful concept in the age of digital reproduction. The entire history of music has been digitally transferred to cyberspace where it exists in an eternal present. It's all there. Every note that's ever been recorded is available, every chord progression, every drum beat, every accidental disharmony . . .'

'Where are you getting this from?'

'I thought it through for myself.'

'Like hell,' Jenny said.

'Oh, all right then,' Trixie trilled, all dimples and tilted head. 'If you must know, I got it from the musical director.'

Jenny couldn't suppress that smouldering streak of jealousy. She should have had that job. There was nobody on God's multicoloured earth who could do it better.

'Does this musical director have a name?' she demanded.

'Tom Scorn,' said Trixie.

Jenny should have known.

Not very much later at all in Tom Scorn's on-set recording studio, Jenny said to him, 'So you're into film music now?'

'I always was,' he said. 'Eric Kornfeld, Bernard Herrmann, they were always my heroes.'

'I thought it was Stockhausen and Cardew.'

'Whatever. The thing is, Jenny, and I've said this before, time is no longer a meaningful concept in the age of digital reproduction . . .'

He ran through the same speech that the child actress had managed to deliver word for word. (Well, at least the kid had the ability to learn lines.) Jenny waited until Scorn came to a part she hadn't heard before.

'If you want to hear Guitar Slim jamming with Yehudi Menuhin,' said Scorn, 'that's easily arranged. We can do that. We can pluck those sounds out of the digital ether. Want to hear what Gary Moore or Johnny Marr sound like improvising over a theme from Purcell? Well no, neither do I, but with technology it's dead easy to achieve. It's all there for the taking by anyone who has some use for it.'

'And you have some use for it?' said Jenny.

'I most certainly do. With a sampler you can take the greatest voices in the whole world – Pavarotti, Joan Sutherland, Tom Waits – and you use just one sampled note, transfer it to a keyboard and instil all the musical qualities of those great artists into your music. You know I'm right.'

'Well,' said Jenny, 'only up to a point.'

Scorn was irritated that anyone should disagree with such clearly irrefutable truths.

'For example,' Jenny said, 'I could write a song with the opening line "I woke up this morning", but that wouldn't necessarily mean I was an authentic blues artist.'

'The concept of the song form is very old hat,' Scorn snarled.

'You can sample Hendrix's guitar tone but it's not as though that makes you Hendrix. It's not even like having Hendrix in the band.'

'Of course it isn't,' Scorn said smugly. 'It's much *better* than having Hendrix in the band. If he were alive today I'd get him into the studio, record five minutes of him jerking around with the guitar and then I'd have no further use for him. I could take that five minutes and do more with it than he did in his whole career.

'Let's face it, live musicians are never anything but pains in the arse. They do too many drugs. They want too much money. They're unreliable, they're temperamental. You can't just tell them to play one chord for fifty minutes, because they think it's uninspired and they want to give of themselves. The sound of Hendrix I love. His genius I love. But having him in the band . . . don't be silly. Give me machines every time.' Then, as an afterthought, 'Did you ever meet Hendrix?'

Jenny said no, but that wasn't strictly true.

AN EXPERIENCE

Jimi slumps on a couch, unconscious, guitar in hand. The couch is decked out with throws and cushions, slices of crushed purple velvet, orange brocade and sequined chiffon. He looks so at home there, like a chameleon gone mad, cheesecloth and love beads, lizard-skin boots, a military tunic, tight cotton trousers patterned with multicoloured Op art squares. And even the guitar matches; an old Strat that's been customized by some fan, some 'psychedelic artist' who's drilled holes in the guitar body, sprayed it with red and black car paint and, while it was running and congealing, stuck rhinestones, rosary beads and silver glitter on to the surface. The process has rendered the guitar more or less unplayable, although Jimi has met a lot of unplayable guitars in his time, and he's usually managed to wring something out of them, which is to say he's used them to wring something out of himself.

Not that he's in any state right this moment to do any playing. He's sleeping the sleep, not of the just, but of the stoned, the sleep of the heavily sedated, the sleep of the totally fucked up. It would take a scientist, a pharmacist, or at the very least a police coroner to tell you what was the exact cause of Jimi's condition. Call it a cocktail, call it a random sample. Jimi gets given all kinds of pharmaceutical treats these days, guys and chicks just lay this really cool stuff on him all the time, and if the precise history, the detailed provenance of most of these drugs is a little blurry, well, that's OK, these people are genuine fans of Jimi. They love him and they love what he does, and they'd have no reason to give him bad shit, no reason to send him on a bad trip, into narcosis and coma. But even if by some mistake they *did* give him some bad stuff, well, Jimi's feeling so strong these days, so big and powerful, so on top and above it all, that bad trips and bad chemicals just bounce off him like rain, or ping-pong balls, or bullets off Superman. Butterfly and bee.

Yeah, he often feels like Superman, or sometimes just a little like Clark Kent, and at other times like Adam Strange or Lex Luther or the Riddler. Funny the way they're all white guys, but the times they are a changin', and maybe he can even do something about that, a black superhero who ain't Muhammad Ali. His dreams are certainly full enough of flying and super powers, of defeating nameless but vibrant-coloured dreads. They're full of big ideas and big insights, heavy shit that you're never going to be able to sit down and explain in words, but with a Strat and a Big Muff and a Uni-Vibe and a wah wah pedal and a Marshall two-hundred-watt stack, well, just maybe you're going to be able to get the message across. So long as you get the right rhythm section.

And some of these dreams come when he isn't even asleep. Like right now he half wakes up and there's this chick standing in the room and he's pretty sure he's never seen her before but she's here and that's groovy, and he can't be absolutely sure that she's not a hallucination or some kind of sweet angel come down. And yeah, maybe she looks a little like Wonderwoman, and she's playing a weird-looking guitar, not one of his, picking out a nice blues, and she looks up and says, 'Now about this stage act of yours, Jimi . . .'

And he's halfway into a conversation he doesn't remember starting.

'Huh?' he says.

'For example, when you mime cunnilingus in the show,' she says, 'or when you masturbate your guitar or bang it on the stage, or when you smash it up or set fire to it . . . what am I supposed to think about that?'

Cogs and cams click in his brain, connect up his speech centres, get the motor running, coming back from out there.

'Well, you know, maybe it's not about *thought*,' he tries. 'It's about just digging it.'

'No, Jimi, that's just not good enough,' she says bossily. 'Of course we all understand the phallic significance of the guitar, but what's the significance of beating your phallus against the stage until it breaks? What's the symbolic value of trying to set your phallus on fire?'

'Gee, I never thought about it quite like that.'

'But I did, Jimi.'

Jimi's face stiffens and she can see that he's rummaging through the files in his head, files that have been chemically shuffled and singed.

'Uh, maybe it's a guy thing, a black thing,' he says. 'I dunno, chicks they don't understand. Hey, why don't you come over here, sit by me, mellow out and stop asking me such hard questions?'

'Women here, women there, always trying to put you in a plastic cage, eh Jimi?'

'Hey, no, I don't mean that exactly. That's just a song, y'know.'

'Is that right? So you don't really think you're a "voodoo chile" or a "hoochie coochie man"?'

'Well, maybe just a little.'

'And are you really saying you're not a "lover man", Jimi?'

He smiles that shy, polite smile, eyes and head turned coyly down. He won't deny it. 'Lady's man, cocksman, axeman, whatever,' he says.

'I thought so,' she says.

'Yeah, sure,' Jimi says. 'It's like a divining rod, maybe a fishing rod. It helps make you feel connected. It helps you make a catch.'

She doesn't bother to ask whether he's talking about his guitar or his penis. It doesn't really matter which.

'It plugs you into these, kinda, energies,' Jimi says. 'And you know out there in swingin' London there's a whole lot of sockets just begging you to plug into them.'

'You always had a way with metaphor, Jimi.'

'Thank you,' he says, hoping he's not being mocked.

'You know,' Jenny says thoughtfully, 'I think that a man generally makes love the same way he plays a guitar solo. For example, some men are very hot and flashy but it's all over in ten seconds. Some make a big noise and it gets the job done but it's crude, simple stuff. Some men are always asking, when's it going to be my turn to take a solo, my turn to perform, as though they're really keen and really good, but when the chance comes and the spotlight's on them they tend to shrivel and lose interest.

'Some other men are very fancy, full of technique and finesse, as though they've read all the books and practised all the moves, but when it comes to the real thing there's no passion there, just a lot of twiddling and showing off to no purpose. What do you think, Jimi?'

He smiles again, a little embarrassed by what he knows he's about to tell her.

'Well,' he says, 'personally, I like to jam and, basically, I'll jam with just about anyone, and once I start jammin' it just goes on and on, hour after hour, sometimes all night long. It gets very free form, very wild, very experimental. I like to get into whole new areas that I've never explored before. I like to try things that I never knew I was capable of. Sometimes it mightn't work out exactly right, but that's cool. I haven't had too many complaints except maybe from the neighbours who start beating on the walls telling me to "keep it down in there", whereas I just want to keep it up.'

He laughs a roguish, boyish laugh and Jenny's inclined to go with it, to be gentle on him, but that's really not what she's there for.

'On the other hand, Jimi, I've never seen too many women in your backing bands.'

'Huh?'

'You know, women keyboard players, women drummers, women bass players. Women who are good for something other than undressing and putting on your album cover.'

'Like I say, I'll play guitar with anyone.'

'Anyone so long as they've got a dick. You're not telling me you couldn't find a woman who played bass better than Billy Cox, better than Noel Redding.'

'Shit, I don't know. Guys are good for playing in bands with. Chicks are good for other things.'

'You know, Jimi, one day soon this kind of talk will sound very sexist.'

'What's that mean?'

'It's a seventies word, Jimi, a seventies concept, but not one that you're going to have to worry too much about.'

'Well, thank God for that.'

'The seventies is going to be a very strange decade for Jimi Hendrix.'

She can see him bristle. Strange is normal where Jimi comes from. He wants the future to be less strange, more structured, more you know, composed.

'Hey,' he says, 'the seventies is going to be a *great* decade for me. I got big plans. I'm going to make some serious music, some serious collaborations, maybe work with Miles Davis, Gil Evans, maybe play with Jeff Beck and John McLaughlin (John's a real spiritual cat), and Eric, of course. Going to make lots of albums, lots of money, put it all together, make a lot of number one hits.'

'The number one hit, yes, you'll have that,' Jenny says cheerfully. 'Thirteen weeks on the chart. The rest of it, I'm afraid not.'

'What you talking about? Who are you to be afraid for me? Who are you anyway? You talk too much to be a groupie. You a fucking journalist or something? You trying to bring me down? You some kind of devil woman?'

194

'As popularized in song?' she says. 'You and Robert Johnson, two of a kind. No, I'm no devil woman. I'm just someone who can see a bit further into the future than you can.'

'You a clairvoyant?'

'No.'

'Or are you just part of a bad trip? You know, I heard there are drugs can give you crazy powers, like telepathy, like the ability to see the future.'

'Drugs are going to kill you, Jimi.'

'Nah, not me. The others. I'm strong. I can take anything.'

'It's OK,' says Jenny. 'A lot of people won't mind you being dead at all. They'll love you for being dead. The seventies, the eighties, the nineties, they're all going to be good decades for James Marshall Hendrix. There'll be lots of respect, adulation, big record sales. There just won't be any more music. Not new music anyway, not by you.'

Jimi looks troubled. He's talked to people who've taken acid and seen visions of their own death. 'Course they ain't necessarily accurate, but it's still scary.

'But a lot of people are going to like that too,' Jenny continues. 'There's nothing like a completed oeuvre to bring out the scholars. But it won't only be scholars. Every guy who ever picks up a guitar is going to try to play the riff from "Purple Haze", and the fact is an awful lot of them are going to get it note-for-note perfect. There are going to be people who spend their whole lives just trying to rip off your sound.'

'You're really starting to bring me down, you know that?' Jimi says.

'I can see how that might happen, Jimi, yes.'

He shudders. He feels a twinge as though someone has snapped a cold guitar string across his back. He doesn't know who this woman is, whether she's flesh or the product of his own mind, but he knows that in some vital sense she's for real. She has a gift, the gift of prophecy, just like in the songs, the legends. This feels like a chillingly authentic blues moment, but also modern, all tuned in with drugs and outer space, stars spangling in the black velvet sky, dead stars, multiple moons. Shit, he's starting to drift away. He hauls himself back.

'You're here to tell me I'm about to die,' he says, just to get this whole thing absolutely clear.

'Yes,' she says.

'And there's nothing I can do about it, right? No penance. No restitution, no second chance.'

'That's it.'

'Boy, that's heavy,' he says.

He thinks, then starts to giggle.

'Hey, maybe you can answer some questions for me.' And suddenly he's wide-eyed and eager for information. 'Is there sex after death? Are there guitars in heaven? Is music like the thing that makes sense of the universe?'

She hasn't the heart to tell him she hasn't the faintest idea, so she tries to be mysterious and says, 'You'll have the answers soon enough.'

Jimi is not deterred. He says, 'Up there you can probably play like for eternity, right? Guitar solos can go on from now until the end of time. I'll get to jam with Charlie Christian and Robert Johnson and all those great guys. Yeah, and new arrivals all the time. I'll eventually get to jam with guys

196

from the future. Play riffs that haven't even been invented yet. Wow. Hey, I'm really getting into this.'

And he starts to laugh and laugh, gets the real giggles, the stoned version that makes no sense but keeps going till it hurts, the cosmic joke, the ultimate laugh track.

'Hey,' he says between bursts of laughter, 'you know there's not much you can tell me about death. I've played the Wolverhampton Gaumont. I've been on tour with the Walker Brothers and Engelbert Humperdinck. Hey, I think there's a song in that, if I could just get this guitar in tune, if I could just get a piece of paper. If I could just wake up.'

Suddenly the room looks dark and he feels all alone. Wasn't there something she was supposed to ask him? His advice for the aspiring guitarist. He has no answer. He knows it has to do with blackness and anger and sex and violence and Vietnam and the ghetto and, yeah, well maybe it's as well she didn't ask. He can tell there are going to be no more songs, no more jams, no guitar solos. Bile wells up in his throat, vomit comes heaving up from his stomach, fills his mouth, his nose, his very being. When he wakes up next morning he finds himself dead.

MORE FILM FUN

So the film got made. They kept changing the title. It went from *Pluck!* to *Twang!* to *Valley of the Plank-Spankers*, compromising with the rather dour title *Plec*. They did a lot of test screenings, messed around with the ending, unable to decide whether the climax should be the heat death of the universe or a song-and-dance number, finally choosing the latter.

Responses were surprisingly good. 'Cool to the max,' was the most frequent comment from white middle-class youth in the cineplexes. A review on the Internet said it was a 'string-driven masterpiece'. The London *Daily Telegraph* called it a 'spirited, youth-orientated extravaganza'. None of these sources said anything at all about the way the actors held their plectrums.

But these were amateur opinions; for a more specialized and authoritative opinion one would naturally have to turn to the *Journal of Sladean Studies*.

Review of *Plec* by Bob Arnold

The opening scene says it all. We're in a plectrum factory, a sweatshop, somewhere in the Third World, somewhere cheap, clean and super-efficient. White-coated workers stand by as gigantic, soulless machines stamp out plectrums by the million. The camera moves along the production line and we see the little plastic suckers being sorted, separated, boxed, despatched. This is a far more significant sequence than the film-makers know. It sets exactly the right tone for a movie that is mechanical, soulless and far too neatly packaged.

Wiser critics than I have raised doubts about the wisdom of selecting the plectrum as a suitable subject for a high-budget three-hour mass-entertainment movie. If the idea sounds tired and jejune, then in Howie Howardson the producers have found a director who was perfectly in tune with the material.

Following the factory sequence we're immediately plunged into Greek antiquity, Lesbos year zero to be precise. Classical scholars may find much to intrigue them here, but for the rest of us it's the nude swimming and dancing sequences that are more likely to grab the attention. Those ancient babes sure knew how to do a lot with a little.

The casting of Sappho was always going to be tricky, and Helen Mirren battles gamely with the role without being utterly convincing. Similarly Eddie Murphy does his best with Henry VIII, but his best just isn't good enough. Some of the cast wrestle bravely with their roles, but they all find themselves pinned to the canvas by a lame, witless, anachronistic script. Other members of the cast don't even seem to be trying. Robert De Niro's depiction of Johnny 'Guitar' Watson suggests that he knows nothing about guitar playing, the blues, or indeed human life on earth.

Strange as it seems, however, especially to me, the one performance that's oddly affecting is that of Trixie Picasso as the young Joan Jett. The scene when her vicious music teacher (edgily played by Dennis Hopper) makes her turn out her pockets and then mocks the presence of the plectrum sent several tears running down my usually poker face. It's a moment that's almost worth the price of admission on its own, but not quite.

As for Jenny Slade's involvement, well, the actors' plectrum technique is fine, certainly better than their acting technique. If anything Megan Floss looks more at home with a plectrum than Patti Smith ever did. On the other hand, Michael Cutlass's macho posturings with a jumbo acoustic suggest that his real instrument is probably the claw hammer.

But you don't have to be Jenny Slade's number one fan to feel that her talents are utterly wasted on this farrago. Why oh why didn't they ask her to write the music, or even have her appear in the film?

Such music as there is comes courtesy of Tom Scorn. His soundtrack is a mess of bass and drum loops, samples, treated vocals and dodgy retro synths. To add insult to injury, acute listeners will be able to spot a sample from Jenny Slade herself (way back in the mix, uncredited, and no doubt unpaid for), which is used in the Link Wray, speaker-piercing sequence. I hope she sues Scorn and the film's producers for everything they've got, although having made this piss poor movie one suspects and indeed hopes that they've got very little.

Journal of Sladean Studies
Volume 9 Issue 2

DEATH AND THE PERCUSSIONIST

Death walks with the guitar player. It is there leaning over
her shoulder as she changes strings. It is there lurking behind
the PA stacks, or surfing in over the heads of the audience.
Death leaves its thick perfume in stinking dressing rooms,
in musty, unopened flight cases. Sometimes it is indistinct,
unfocused, as unformed and shapeless as a forty-five-minute
blues jam, but other times it shapes up, gets its act together,
does the business.

Jenny Slade used to say she wished she could have been
there on 26 November 1973 when John Rostill of the
Shadows was found in his own studio apparently electrocuted by his guitar. The coroner returned an open verdict,
but Jenny didn't like things to be that open. She wanted to
close the case, to know the full story. Rostill was not the
only one. Keith Relf, of the Yardbirds, he too was found
dead at home clutching a live guitar, and he didn't even
consider himself a guitarist.

But death likes to get away from home, to go on the road,
to get on the bus and tour. It has a sense of the big occasion,
an unfailing grasp of showbiz. Death enjoys playing to the
gallery. All sorts of players, from Gary Thain of Uriah Heep

to Bill Wyman and Keith Richards, have received monster electric shocks on stage, but they all survived. However, death really put on a show on 3 May 1972 with Les Harvey, guitar player in Stone the Crows. He was electrocuted live on stage in front of an audience of 1200 at the Top Rank, Swansea. You can't follow that.

These deaths which are so appropriate, so fitting, so electric, can make the more usual musicians' deaths seem positively tame and beside the point. Drink, drugs, choking on vomit, plane crashes, Aids, even blowing your own head off, somehow they lack the mythic structure of a death that comes to you direct through the very medium that makes the music possible.

And at least it's quick. If nothing else, an early death must surely save you from a long, slow, lingering one. It may not simply be a question of rusting or fading but rather of lasting long enough to fall prey to the old horrors, the old men's illnesses. But few have suffered so badly or so early as Jon Churchill who was diagnosed as suffering from Alzheimer's disease when he was barely forty-five years old.

Jon had started out as an exceptionally youthful jazz and big band drummer, but he was young enough and smart enough to reinvent himself as a rock and roller by the time of the Beatles and sixties beat groups. He was much in demand as a session man and though he was too cool ever to name names, he never denied the rumours that he was the drummer on twenty or more Merseybeat hit singles. This despite his having been born and raised in Great Yarmouth.

Then, in the early seventies, he joined a power trio called Dreadnought, who played distinctly ponderous heavy rock, gathered terrible reviews, but nevertheless made a terrific pile of money touring the States and the Far East. The band was so successful that Churchill was able to indulge a taste for more esoteric playing, and he and Jenny Slade performed and recorded some truly off-the-wall duets.

Twenty years on, Dreadnought records were still selling massively and the band were still having occasional and highly profitable reunion tours, and it was on one of these that the Alzheimer's first got to Jon.

It was during a second encore at the Dallas Civic Arena, playing a famous Dreadnought number called 'The Journey', a complex, twenty-minute multi-sectioned workout that he knew like the back of his hand, when he suddenly forgot what song he was playing. He also forgot what city he was in, who the two guys on stage with him were, and if anybody had asked he'd have been hard pressed to come up with his own name or even what planet he was on.

Afterwards, when he was back to normal, he wanted to put it down to road fever, to too many late nights, to too many drugs taken many years ago, but he got himself to a doctor who told him it was Alzheimer's, and also assured him there was no coming back, no way out of the tunnel.

Jon Churchill went into distinguished semi-retirement, stopped playing in public, but fortunately was still in demand for session work. He played on a Pete Townshend solo project, was the house drummer for a session at a guitar festival in Seville. He played free jazz with Derek Bailey and Evan Parker, worked with Ryan Beano, Steve Albini, Laurie Anderson and, of course, Jenny Slade. He was still highly respected, and he was lucky. For a long time the bad, blank phases never coincided with important studio dates. But when a furious Daniel Lanois rang up demanding to know why Churchill wasn't at a session in New Orleans, Jon denied all knowledge of the booking, of the music he was supposed to have learned, and before the end of the phone call he'd also forgotten who he was talking to.

A part of him was still intelligent and thoughtful and so he decided to stop right there, to slip away gracefully. There was a small farewell charity gig, in front of an invited audience, at which he played faultlessly along with a lot of the usual suspects. Sting sent his apologies, but Kim Gordon and Ray Cooper made it. It was a good gig and there was a live CD, although the sales were admittedly disappointing.

After that he gave up drumming completely and retired to a converted lifeboat station on the Suffolk coast. He said he would never bother or embarrass anybody with his condition. He would not ask for sympathy nor rub his illness in anyone's face, and he was as good as his word.

It was a big change for his wife Beth. She was a session singer in her own right and had recently started to perform with a jazz a cappella group, but she had no hesitation in giving that up and agreeing to this strange new life. She would be there to protect him from the world. There would be no visitors, no journalists. He would be allowed to slip slowly and permanently from the public imagination.

It was a quiet life. Jon Churchill would spend most of his days sitting on the porch of the house, watching the sea. Often he felt adrift as the tides of dementia swept in and made his mind as smooth and clear as sand, then later, more terrifyingly, he would have moments of clarity and realize how much he'd lost, how much he still had to lose. He sometimes glanced at the newspapers, though the affairs of the world meant nothing to him, and sometimes he would listen to music, even on occasions his own music, but that too made little impression.

His old drum kit was kept in the basement of the house. Since the charity gig Jon had not shown the slightest inclination to play the drums, had even suggested to Beth that they sell them. But Beth hadn't allowed that and so the drums remained in the cellar, still and silent, along with his collection of percussion instruments from around the world. There was plenty of the more orthodox stuff, the tambourines and maracas, congas, bongos and tom toms, marimbas and castanets. But then there were more ethnic instruments; thumb pianos, talking drums, log drums, tablas, a derbuka. There was electronic gadgetry: pads, kick controllers, acoustic triggers. And then there were lots of items he'd built himself: weird percussive devices made from springs, car parts, beer cans, the insides of typewriters and old computers. Sometimes Beth would go down and look at it all and she couldn't help weeping, but for Jon none of it had any more emotional significance than a new drumskin.

Beth was determined not to treat her husband like an invalid, and not to turn herself into a nursemaid. There was no need. His body remained fit and strong and he was in no danger of injuring himself. He could certainly be left on his own without her needing to worry. So she often drove into town for the day and did some shopping, bought food for the house and one or two things for herself. She might buy some expensive and impractical article of clothing that she would never have any occasion to wear, and perhaps half a dozen new paperbacks that she would read in the long quiet evenings.

It was on just such a day, an overcast, blustery day in early summer, after she'd been gone for four hours or so, that she returned to find that something quite extraordinary had happened in her absence. A profound change had overcome her husband.

At first, as she pulled into the drive of the house, she could see and hear nothing different, but then she turned off the car engine and she heard drumming. There was no mistaking Jon's style, and the quality of the sound told her it was live, not recorded. She ran round the side of the house and peered in through the french doors. Jon Churchill was indeed playing the drums. He'd moved his kit and all his percussion instruments up from the basement to the living room, and as he played his face looked utterly vacant and his eyes stared out at the sea and sky. His playing was rhythmic but slow, determined yet not thunderous. Beth didn't know whether to weep or to cheer, and in the event she did a little of both.

Jon saw her standing on the other side of the glass and, without missing a beat, motioned for her to come inside. The day was chilly and the sea was loud and as Beth opened the french doors cold air and the steady, shuffling sound of the sea rolled into the room. A look of wonder came into Jon's eyes and he began to play in time with the noise of the sea. Six hours later he was still playing, and he didn't stop until eventually he fell asleep sitting up on his drum stool.

Thus began the worst month of Beth's life. Night and day, all day, every day, every minute except when he was eating or sleeping (and he did little of either) Jon Churchill continued to play the drums. A part of Beth was pleased, or at least felt she ought to be pleased, for when Jon played it was as though he was his old self again. He had lost none of his touch or dexterity. On one level she could even appreciate his performance, for this wasn't just doodling or practising, he was performing as though for an audience, and although he seemed to be playing a drum solo of indefinite, possibly infinite, length there was a recognizable shape and structure to what he was doing. He was improvising and yet his playing seemed thought out, fully conceived, composed even. He never paused to consider what to do next.

Beth had always loved his drumming, the way his body moved when he played, the supple articulation of his sound. And yet who could possibly live in the same house as a man who played the drums relentlessly for eighteen or twenty hours a day?

Their nearest neighbour lived at least a quarter of a mile away, which was fortunate in one sense. There was nobody to bang on the walls or call the police. On the other hand it meant that Beth was totally alone in her ordeal. The cleaning woman came, listened to Jon playing the drums, seemed appreciative and told Beth she thought this was a terribly good sign. But she only had to live with it for an hour a day and Beth suspected that what she really appreciated was the fact that she didn't have to clean the living room.

Beth, needless to say, did occasionally ask her husband to stop playing; at bedtime for instance, at mealtimes, when she wanted to watch something on television. Jon didn't say no. He didn't argue or defy her. He simply failed to communicate with her at all, and carried on drumming. Of course she got angry with him. Of course she shouted at him, but it did no good. He acted as though he hadn't heard and, in truth, when his drumming hit a particularly loud patch, she could barely hear herself.

Every moment of Beth's life was now filled with the sound of her husband's drumming. Her every move and thought was accompanied by cymbal crashes, flams, rolls, para-diddles, ruffs, rim shots. Some moments were quieter than others. There were times when he played with brushes, or tapped out extraordinarily complex figures solely on the ride cymbal. Occasionally he'd sit with a tambourine in one hand and a shaker in the other, and spend twenty or thirty minutes exploring their tonal and rhythmic possibilities. But he never completely stopped playing, and Beth knew that these moments of comparative peace would invariably resolve themselves into louder, more aggressive, truly intolerable bursts of percussion.

At first she thought he must eventually wear himself out. She thought he would either run out of ideas or stop because of simple physical exhaustion. It was true that he did sleep sometimes, either on the stool, as on that first night, or on the couch in the corner of the room. But these naps were short, infrequent, taken at peculiar times of the day, and he would wake suddenly, perfectly refreshed and begin playing with renewed vigour and vehemence.

When Beth started to feel positively suicidal she called the one person she hoped might be able to help. But Sting was still busy and she had to fall back on Jenny Slade. She called her and begged her for help. Jenny turned up at the house the next day with her guitar, a couple of pedals and a small tube amp, and after a long talk with Beth she went into the room where Jon Churchill was still playing and she set up her equipment.

If Jon recognized Jenny from the old days he certainly did nothing to indicate the fact. Indeed her presence in the room seemed to be a matter of complete indifference to him. He showed neither interest nor surprise and when Jenny cranked her guitar into life and began to play along with him, he looked as though he was completely oblivious to the noise she was making. And yet something was happening. After half an hour or so the music began to gel. He was not making any concessions to her guitar playing, but gradually the dynamics of the music changed. Soon she was no longer just playing along with him; they were definitely playing together.

There were some rough edges, moments when they lost each other, but there was no doubt that a terrific interaction was taking place. A strange and complex piece of music was coming into being there in the living room of this Suffolk beach house. After two hours had passed, two hours of the most intense, intricate, draining invention on Jenny's part, she needed a rest. She unhooked her guitar, turned off the amp, but Jon went right on playing.

Beth and Jenny walked along the straight shingle beach together, far enough away from the house so that they could no longer hear the drumming.

'Oh well,' said Beth, 'it was a nice try. I thought a face

from the old days might bring him back to normal. Shame it didn't work.'

'What are you talking about?' Jenny replied. 'It worked beautifully. Jon and I are going to create a lot of beautiful music before we're finished. Maybe it'll be his last gasp, maybe it won't quite work, but I think we're going to have a great work of art on our hands.'

'But how can it be art?' Beth demanded. 'Art demands consciousness, discrimination, a guiding personality. Poor Jon doesn't have any of those things. He's just playing through sheer instinct. I don't think he has a clue what he's doing.'

'Maybe not,' Jenny agreed. 'But *I* do, and it would be criminal to let it just slip away. I'll have a mobile recording van here as soon as humanly possible. I don't want to miss a single beat more than I have to.'

Beth shook her head sadly. This was not what she'd had in mind at all, and yet she couldn't deny that Jenny Slade was probably doing the right thing. Perhaps her husband's music did deserve preserving and recording, but that didn't help her to find it any less intolerable.

Jenny made a couple of phone calls before returning for another two-hour session with Jon that night. Beth sat on the grass in the garden, pulling the heads off dandelions. As well as her husband's drumming she now had to contend with a hundred decibels of distorted guitar noise. She got little sleep that night, but at least she was awake next morning when the mobile studio arrived in her front garden and youths with shaved heads began laying cables all around the house.

Jon Churchill drummed on oblivious to the mikes and screens that were being set up around him. He was of no use to anyone in helping to create a good drum sound, but neither did he hinder or object to what they were doing. When the engineers were happy with the balance, they miked Jenny into the board and the recordings began. These tapes, which were later to be dubbed *The Dementia Sessions*, are generally agreed to be some of the most intense, most extreme drum and guitar duets ever recorded.

Jenny Slade and Jon Churchill played together with only the most perfunctory breaks and interruptions for the best part of seventy-two hours. Jenny stopped once in a while to retune or to modify her guitar tone, and to replace the occasional broken string, but Jon just kept playing through the gaps.

There was certainly a development as the days progressed. The music of the first day was taut and disciplined in a way that would seem staid compared with the later stuff. The music, without ever losing its focus, became increasingly loose, free form, untrammelled. It became wilder and more Dionysian as it went on, but it never sounded chaotic, never lost its way or its sense of itself. Certain passages were remarkably simple and lyrical, just a simple four-note guitar melody played against a repeated drum pattern. At other times both players displayed a breathtaking, bravura virtuosity.

Later Bob Arnold would write, 'Few people have been lucky enough to hear the entire session from beginning to end, but those who have are stunned by the work's essential unity and coherence. Rhythms and chord progressions that are quickly passed over in the early hours of the session are reworked and given full expression some twenty or thirty hours later. The three-CD set that was extracted from the tapes represents a distillation but also an enormous reduction. The complete work derives its strength and majesty from its sheer size and scale, and in a perfect world it would always be listened to as a whole.'

Given the way the recording was set up, it inevitably started *in medias res*, at the moment when the engineers happened to be ready, and the ending was similarly abrupt and arbitrary. After three days of continuous playing, Jenny was more than ready to call it quits. It was only Jon Churchill's relentless energy, her fear of letting him down, and her sense that she was part of something so very important that had kept her going for so long.

When Jon Churchill suddenly stopped, threw down his sticks and walked out through the french doors, she felt nothing but relief. She followed him, hoping that he might at last have something to say to her, some comment to make on what they'd been creating. In the event she was disappointed. He ran off down the beach and she was far too weary to chase after him. Dan, one of the engineers, offered her a beer and a bacon sandwich and that more than absorbed her attention. The crew turned off the recording gear and took a desperately needed break.

It was then that Jenny Slade spoke briefly to Beth. It had been a tough few days for everyone, but Beth looked particularly shattered and demented by it all.

'This is not what I wanted,' Beth said, and she wandered off, amazed that silence had finally fallen on her house, and walked into the living room as though to savour the peace and quiet there, but she didn't stay long.

Jenny didn't know whether the session was over or not. If Jon Churchill had come back from the beach and taken up his place behind the drums she would certainly have joined him. But he was away a long time and on his return he entered the house through a side door, thus avoiding everyone, and he went into the living room, to the makeshift studio and picked up Jenny's guitar, slung it round his neck and turned on the power to the amp.

The electric shock must have come immediately, since nobody heard him play any notes or chords. Instead he received a bolt of electric current that threw him across the room and dumped him on top of his drum kit.

The noise from the amp, followed by the sudden crash, the noise of colliding drums and guitar was truly terrible, and it was immediately obvious that something bad had happened, and even though Beth raced into the room, turned off the power and began immediate first aid, somehow everyone knew it was a futile exercise. Jon Churchill was killed by electricity in his own living room having played the most extraordinary music of his life.

There are those who say it was a merciful death, a quick, clean release from the lingering horrors of Alzheimer's, and there are those who say he engineered the death himself. Perhaps he had deliberately got his hands wet on the beach. Perhaps he had interfered with the power supply, certainly some of the cables were frayed and worn, and Dan the engineer swore they hadn't been like that when he'd first connected them. Jenny examined her guitar and amp and was all too aware that Jon's death might very easily have been hers. The fatal shock had been there waiting for whoever picked up the guitar.

Beth was inconsolable, hysterical, half out of her mind with grief and exhaustion. She would scream at Jenny, blaming her for the death, saying it was all her fault, and then she would crumple with misery and say it was all her *own* fault. Everyone assured her that she mustn't blame herself, but it did little good.

After the ambulance and the doctor and the police had gone there was nothing left for Jenny and the crew to do but pack up and go home. Dan the engineer was unusually quiet and broody. The death seemed to have affected him profoundly despite his never have met Jon Churchill until the beginning of the session. Jenny tried to console him but he didn't want to be consoled.

'I have no right to call myself an engineer,' he berated himself. 'The first rule of recording is to always keep the tape running. And I didn't. That noise, the sound from the guitar when it electrocuted him, that drum crash, if only I could have got that on tape, I'd have made a fucking fortune.'

Jenny slapped him hard across the face with a bundle of twisted guitar leads and made her own way home.

CAGED SKRONK

Tom Scorn drove himself to the San Germano Correctional Facility; a high-tech, high-security prison, thick, high Victorian walls, built in the middle of swamp and wasteland, where he was booked to do a solo gig, part of a rehabilitation scheme. He pulled up at the electronic gate and showed the necessary documents to a guard in a black uniform spattered with red fringes and braid, and was waved through to a central courtyard. Two more uniformed men took his equipment out of the van for him and he was conducted through a sort of portcullis into a metal chamber where he found yet another guard. This one was apparently higher ranking, the uniform more ornate.

'Ready for the strip search?' the guard asked nonchalantly.

'Actually, no,' Scorn replied.

'It's just a formality,' said the guard. 'We know what musicians are like.'

'You really think I'm going to come in here carrying drugs?'

'Drugs is the least of it,' the guard said, still cheery.

Scorn saw no point fighting. If you wanted to play to a gaol full of dangerous criminals then you had to make some compromises. Having nothing to hide, he started to undo the buttons of his shirt.

'Hey, I'll do that,' the guard shouted, and he made Scorn remain motionless as the clothes were peeled from him.

The guard was brisk, without being rough, thorough without being invasive. He found plenty of opportunity to lay his hands on Scorn's body and the red fringing of his uniform brushed repeatedly against Scorn's bare flesh.

'What sort of music do you play exactly?' he asked.

'Well,' said Scorn thoughtfully, 'it's certainly not easy music. It's challenging, thought-provoking. It makes the listener reassess his own position with regard to the world, as does all art, of course.'

'A bit like that Jenny Slade, then.'

'Not entirely unlike her, I suppose,' Scorn said drily.

'We tried to get her to come here but the governor thought it was asking for trouble bringing a woman to play in a men's prison.'

Scorn grunted.

'Well, good luck,' the guard said. 'You might need it.' He peered inquisitively into Scorn's holes and crevices and said, 'OK, you're clean.'

'I *know*,' Scorn replied.

He put his clothes on. The guard dusted him down, slapped him on the buttock and accompanied him through an electronic door into a featureless corridor beyond.

'You'll be playing in the Beckett Theatre,' the guard said.

Scorn had already been told this, although he didn't know and couldn't quite imagine what kind of theatre they were likely to have in a high-security prison. Maybe the talk of fierce discipline was exaggerated. Maybe in reality it was all concert parties and amateur dramatics.

'There have been some spectacular acts performed in the Beckett Theatre,' the guard remarked. 'The place has quite a history. It dates back to the time when the San Germano was a hospital and madhouse.'

'Hospital?' Scorn repeated, light suddenly dawning. 'It's not an operating theatre is it?'

The guard laughed at the very idea. 'Of course it's not,' he said brightly. 'It's a former dissection theatre.'

Before Scorn could express surprise they had arrived. Two wooden swing doors were set in the steel-lined corridor and the guard pushed him through into the theatre. It was reminiscent of a bear pit. The space was circular, not large, with steeply rising banks of seats on all sides. The 'stage' where the dissections would once have taken place was in the centre, the performances here would always be 'in the round'. The dissection table had gone but there was a distinctly medical air to what had been left behind: white tiles, a sluice and overhead illumination as fierce as searchlights. There was not going to be much of an atmosphere, Scorn thought, and the acoustics were bound to be horrible.

'Nervous?' the guard asked.

'A little,' Scorn confessed. 'I think a few nerves help improve a performance.'

'Yeah, well I'd have nerves too if I was going to stand up on my own in front of a roomful of druggies, murderers and bum bandits.'

The two guards who'd taken Scorn's equipment now arrived and set down the four electronic keyboards and amplifiers that he was using for his set. There was also a small, square card table, whose function at this stage was obscure. Scorn set up the gear himself, while the guards watched him with bored curiosity. Ostensibly they were here to help, to provide what he needed, but when he asked for a cup of coffee or a bottle of mineral water all three assured him these were unrealistic and unrealizable requests. Scorn got the impression that the guards were there as his captors rather than his protectors.

Soon sounds came from the corridor outside and the captive audience began to arrive. They shuffled into the theatre and took their places in the wooden seats. They seemed reluctant, repressed, as though they had been dragged there unwillingly, as though attendance at this concert was just another aspect of their continuing punishment. Certainly, Scorn noted with some relief, there appeared to be enough guards in attendance to ensure the prisoners behaved themselves.

He was used to facing an audience, but this time half of them were behind him, and he could feel their hostile stares boring into his back. He was also accustomed to waiting for an audience to settle down and quieten before he started playing but this audience was already absolutely silent and still.

The piece he had decided to play was called 'Absent Kings', one of his more recent, and in his opinion, less demanding compositions. The performance began as he produced a pack of playing cards, removed the four kings and tossed them into the audience. This caused the most muted of ripples. He then dealt out the rest of the pack face-down on the card table. He paused theatrically, then turned over the first card, looked at it briefly and ran to one of the keyboards where he played a single note of D.

The composition fell broadly into the category of 'systems music' and someone familiar with the genre might instantly have realized what Scorn was up to. Each card on the table represented a note of the chromatic scale of A, so that an ace was A, 2 was A sharp, 3 was B, 4 was C, and so on: twelve cards per suit corresponding to the twelve musical notes. Each of the four suits in turn corresponded to each of the four keyboards on stage, so that if Scorn turned up a heart he'd have to play on keyboard number one, a spade meant keyboard number two, a diamond was number three and so on, each keyboard having a different, though equally cheap and cheerful, tone. Thus if he dealt the cards three of diamonds, queen of hearts, eight of clubs, he would have to play B on the third keyboard, then G sharp on the first keyboard, followed by E on the fourth keyboard. The keyboards were deliberately set just out of reach of each other so he had to dash from one to another leaving silences between each note. The music was thrillingly spare and thin.

The sight and sound of Scorn dashing around the stage playing apparently random notes might have appealed to a fan of the more ironic avant-garde. It might even have caused gentle amusement to those with a sense of the ridiculous. However the prison population at the San Germano Correction Facility contained neither of those types. After thirty or forty seconds of 'Absent Kings' the audience in the Beckett Theatre erupted in passionate, violent booing.

The prisoners were on their feet shouting, heckling,

cat-calling. The prison guards tried to remain unmoved and unimpressed by the reaction, but that was a difficult act to pull off. They suddenly looked terribly outnumbered and ineffectual.

Scorn, who had never been one to seek easy audience approval, thought there was something rather wonderful about the directness and vehemence of the response, and he was still feeling that way when the prisoners rushed the stage, knocking prison guards unconscious as they came. They seized Scorn and dragged him out of the theatre. As he lay on the floor in the corridor outside he could hear the sound of his keyboards being smashed to pieces, but he tended to think this too was a valid aesthetic response, and he was still having these charitable thoughts as he was kicked into unconsciousness.

A scrum formed around him and he was manhandled into the toilet block, while other prisoners engaged in a pitched battle with the guards. There was an amount of wounding and maiming on both sides, and honours remained even in terms of combat, but having Tom Scorn as a hostage gave the prisoners a definite edge. Before long a state of siege obtained throughout the prison and the circus could begin in earnest.

Outside the walls armed police arrived in numbers, along with a crack negotiating team, some SAS men, fleets of heli-copters and armoured cars, ambulances, fire engines. And of course the media came too, teams of reporters and film and television crews, along with a throng of amateur gawpers who'd braved the swamp and wasteland to be there.

Communication was established with the prisoners and

after some hours of intense, complex see-sawing negoti-ations, the prisoners finally made their demands clear.

Jenny Slade was watching the whole thing on TV, thinking that it couldn't happen to a nicer guy than Tom Scorn. She hadn't touched her guitar since the death of Jon Churchill. Music seemed an all too melancholy activity. That was when she got a phone call from a senior member of the negotiating team, one Major Warren. His voice was clipped, unemo-tional, narrow in range. She somehow assumed he had a trim toothbrush moustache.

'They're desperate men,' he said of the prisoners. 'If we put a foot wrong they wouldn't think twice about killing Tom Scorn.'

'Well, I've thought about it at least once, myself.'

'I beg your pardon.'

'The man's a fool,' Jenny said drily. 'What did he want to play that experimental stuff for? When *I* get invited to play in a prison I always do some country and western songs. "Coward of the County" generally goes down pretty well.'

'It's funny you should say that,' the major said, 'because that's more or less what we've got in mind.'

'Huh?'

'Actually it wasn't what I personally had in mind at all. I rather favoured the use of nerve gas, but that's just me. The situation is this; the prisoners will release Tom Scorn on one condition only – that you play a concert for them.'

Jenny Slade found this completely mad. There were surely easier ways of getting a change in the entertainment. Why would they risk so much? But mad or not, when the request was put to her so directly how could she refuse? She supposed that on balance she didn't want to be responsible for Tom Scorn's death, so she would do what was required, but it still seemed to be an arrangement full of problems.

'If I go in there to play a gig, what's to say they won't kidnap me as well? They could end up with two hostages instead of one.'

'We've discussed that of course, Ms Slade,' the major said suavely. 'The prisoners themselves have suggested that you play outside the prison, on a patch of waste ground in front of the main gate. Now, there's a slight problem here since the prison is rather well soundproofed but we've talked to an expert, a technical boffin, and he swears he's got some special highly penetrative amplification equipment that means they'll be able to hear clear as a bell in there. The boffin's name is Tubby Moran.'

'The man who invented Bliss?' Jenny said.

'Well, I'm not sure I'd go that far.'

Jenny gave her consent, and while pantechnicons moved masses of unfamiliar sound equipment to the site, Jenny practised a few Hank Williams and Patsy Cline favourites. She suspected this was going to be a very weird gig.

Jenny was driven to the prison, accompanied by motorcycle outriders. The hastily built stage outside the prison was small, but the surrounding structure of amplifiers and speakers was overwhelming. It looked like the ruined gateway to some futuristic city. Parts of it were recognizable as standard stage rig, but whole chunks were quite unlike anything she'd ever seen before. There were clusters of ominous, curling tubes, and vast metal plates and crude square

222

horns and cones mounted on scaffolding towers. Much of it looked like debris from a scrapyard and Jenny hoped that was all it was, junk sculpture, but there was something forbidding and brutal about it, that suggested more than just decoration. And there, at the centre, dressed in camouflage gear, directing operations, climbing over the structure and snarling instructions through a surprisingly crude-looking megaphone, was Tubby Moran.

'Hi kid,' he said, when he saw Jenny.

'So this is what you're into now, is it?' Jenny asked. 'No more drugs, no more Bliss, no more production deal?'

'I'm still into all those things,' he said, 'but *this* is the future.'

He waved grandly at the equipment.

'Music isn't just about leisure and pleasure,' he said. 'It's more elemental than that. Plug into the right frequencies and it's the very stuff of the universe.'

Ignoring this high-falutin' tone, Jenny asked, 'What *is* all this gear? It looks like a war zone.'

'Don't worry your pretty little head about that,' Moran replied. 'You just play. Leave the hardware to me. You just be the software.'

Once again Jenny felt she had no choice. She took her guitar, plugged in and strummed. The sound was nice, surprisingly clean and conventional considering the outlandishness of the set up. It sounded like an old classic tube amp. The bass was particularly thick and rich.

This was not the kind of show where there would be a support act, not even a master of ceremonies. All around the stage there were soundmen, police, reporters, plenty of people watching, even some soldiers, but when she began to play a version of 'Tie A Yellow Ribbon' she knew she was doing it mostly for an invisible and incarcerated audience.

She had been playing no more than a minute and a half when she saw that one or two of the policemen were looking very unsteady on their feet, then one of them gripped his stomach and started to retch. Before long she could see that everyone within hearing distance of the stage seemed to be having breathing difficulties, falling to their knees, collapsing in pain.

Tubby Moran was on stage beside her, looking horribly pleased with himself.

'Ah, the potency of cheap music,' he said.

'What's going on?' Jenny demanded.

'Infrasound,' he said. 'Sound waves below twenty hertz, very low frequency, below what the human ear can hear. But the fact you can't hear it doesn't mean it isn't effective. Mild exposure causes giddiness and nausea. At high density it cracks walls.'

Jenny stared at him in horror and she suddenly began to understand. 'Of course, you can't just walk up to a prison wall with an infrasound generator,' Moran continued. 'So the challenge was to find a way of combining the infrasound with the notes of an electric guitar. We also had to devise a way of shielding the stage from the infrasound so that the guitar player didn't suffer the same effects and could carry on playing. I think I can say that today we've solved those problems.'

Jenny stopped playing, wanting to put an end to the

224

sound, but Moran signalled to one of his back-stage crew who threw some switches. A squall of feedback grew and swelled from Jenny's guitar, regardless of anything she did to it. She had heard louder guitar noise, had indeed played it herself, but never with such results. Suddenly it was as though the towering stone walls of the prison had been turned to cardboard. A rip appeared from top to bottom, at first just a few inches wide, but stretching all the time until it was wide enough to let a man pass through it, at which point various prisoners did just that.

They straggled out in single file holding a tattered, bruised Tom Scorn in front of them as a shield. They started piling into the trucks that had delivered the sound equipment, ready to make a getaway, and the police and military just sat back, too sick to do anything about it.

The guitar howl played on, the gap continued to widen and prisoners continued to pour out. What happened next was inevitable; at least Jenny could see it coming all too clearly. She couldn't bear to look, yet she couldn't turn away as the gap finally got so wide that the whole wall of the prison quaked and then collapsed.

In the panic that followed, Jenny was able to silence her guitar. That was when the forces of law and order moved in. There were smoke bombs and semi-automatic fire, water cannons, crack teams of SAS boys scampering up and down the crumbling masonry of the prison, grenade explosions, clouds of tear gas. When the fog of war had thinned, it was apparent that the vans full of prisoners had gone, along with Tubby Moran and his crew. It was apparent too that quite a few men had died in the collapse of the prison, both guards and inmates, and Tom Scorn was found trussed, his throat cut with a guitar string, his every orifice having been used for acts both conventional and experimental.

Months later the official inquiry asserted that mistakes had been made at the San Germano Correctional Facility. The regime at the prison, it was declared, had been too harsh in certain areas, too soft in others. There were lessons to be learned. The practice of allowing live entertainment in prison was immediately halted, and easy-listening programmes were piped into every cell in every gaol in the country, to soothe and sedate the captive population. The question of how and why Tubby Moran had been able to use infrasound to enact the gaolbreak was regarded as too sensitive and secret to be publicly discussed. However, an appendix to the report argued that there was a case for licensing the electric guitar, like a gun or a Rottweiler, and that unlicensed or dangerous users should be heavily fined.

The report exonerated Tom Scorn, easy enough since he was now something of a martyr, but was rather less forgiving of Jenny Slade. While she was clearly not the prime mover in the gaolbreak she was certainly in some sense the cause. And although she appeared not to have committed any indictable offence, in the absence of the actual culprit, she was a very convenient scapegoat and a certain amount of the mud thrown at her was bound to stick.

For her part, Jenny felt thoroughly, desperately guilty. Yes, she knew Tubby Moran was the real villain but that didn't make her feel any better. Men had died when the walls came tumbling down, and even among survivors the after-effects of infrasound were grisly and long lasting. It wasn't an event you could just shrug off.

Jenny was much written and talked about. Other stories about her started to make the papers. Most of them were pretty old and careworn, stories about the ruination of the Hormone Twins, about the deaths of Captain Ahab and Jon Churchill. There were even fabricated stories about the Daughters of Jenny Slade, who supposedly cut off a hand in honour of their heroine. In more perverse reports the hand had been transformed into a breast.

At first Jenny read the stories as though they referred to someone else, someone foul and vicious, someone she wouldn't choose to be in the same room with, much less choose to be. She knew it was rumours and lies and stories they'd made up, but before long, perversely, she couldn't help believing there must be some truth in them. Late in the day she began to believe her own press. A fathomless and unshakeable melancholy enfolded her like a poncho.

In the world of rock and roll it is often said that no publicity is bad publicity, yet there was no doubt that after the events at the prison Jenny Slade found it much harder to get gigs, and when she got them the audiences were smaller, their responses depressingly muted. Her confidence began to falter. She wondered if it had all been sound and fury. Perhaps her whole career had been merely a hiccup in popular taste. She'd fooled some of the people for some of the time, but that time had now passed.

She began to play safe, to anaesthetize and protect herself: drink and drugs helped a little, as did long hours locked away indoors. She cried a lot, and not only when she was alone. She wept all the way through a recording session where she was supposed to be providing racy, upbeat rock guitar for a soft drink commercial. She cancelled some of her gigs; at others she simply failed to show up. When she *did* show up she was often in no condition to play. If she *did* manage to play she'd almost certainly perform badly and alienate the audience.

She began to wish the piano had been her instrument. A piano player who was past it and past caring could always get a gig, even if it was only tinkling the ivories in some cocktail lounge, like Walter Hormone. But a state of the art experimentalist who had stopped experimenting, who had stopped caring about her art, was no use to anyone.

She turned up at a few jam sessions, made a fool of herself by playing insanely loud, fast, tuneless solos during soulful renditions of 'The Thrill Is Gone'. If she was tolerated at all it was as a kind of joke, an eccentric comedy act, but those who had known her at her best found it a sad, sick joke.

Every time she picked up the guitar she died a little. She wouldn't have minded going like Jon Churchill, would have been perfectly happy to die on stage, to add the literal death to the metaphoric. But that didn't happen.

She felt cursed. And maybe it went all the way back. Perhaps it wasn't Ahab who had lured the Magic Big Band to its doom all those years ago, but her. She was the affliction, the bird of ill omen.

And she began to think that maybe Tom Scorn had been right when he said the days of the musician were over. Maybe it would be machines from now on, machines capable of tireless precision. Maybe the electric guitar was a remnant of a closed period of history, like the hurdy-gurdy or the serpent.

When things were looking their very worse she got a letter from someone who claimed to be her number one fan, saying that she must carry on playing, get back to being her old self. There was a fanzine enclosed. It reported in dreary detail all the facts of her recent musically and spiritually bad gigs. She didn't need reminding and threw the magazine away. She looked at the signature on the letter, 'Bob Arnold, your number one fan'. She'd never heard of him. She tore the letter into obsessively small, neat pieces and burned them.

She became a recluse. She grew her nails long. Her career seemed to be over and she had no complaints, no regrets. Silence beckoned and she welcomed it, but she wasn't content to slide into easy retirement. She needed to go out with a bang, not the ordinary sort of bang, not the farewell tour, not the 'Best of' album. She wanted to play just one last time, to hit it and quit, and she knew the very place to do it, a place at the end of the world, where the rules didn't apply, a place where she wasn't known, where the audience was hostile and the PA useless: the Havoc Bar and Grill.

LAST DISORDERS

'Look, it's really very late and I've quite enjoyed talking to you,' Kate says to Bob Arnold, 'but I've got to close up the bar now. Stop by again. Tomorrow's another day, you know.'

'That's undeniably true,' says Bob.

'And who knows, maybe it'll be a day when you can catch Jenny Slade's act again.'

This time he really does bang his head against the bar. He lets it drop like a bag of potatoes and although it lands with a sickening crack, Bob is sufficiently drunk not to feel the pain.

'There won't be any gig tomorrow,' he says desperately. 'Nor the day after that. Haven't I made myself clear? Jenny Slade played her last ever gig here, a few hours ago, and I didn't see it. *You* saw it. A crowd of drunken hoi polloi, *they* saw it. But *I*, the number one Jenny Slade fan in the whole world, I didn't.'

'Her last gig, wow. I can see why missing it would depress you.'

'Depress!' he says it as though the word cannot express a millionth part of the anguish and misery he is still feeling.

This isn't just a heartache. It isn't just a mild case of the summertime blues.

'But why would she choose this dump for her farewell gig?' Kate asks.

'Precisely because it was a dump,' Bob explains. 'Because it wasn't on the map. She didn't want her fans there, didn't want a loyal following, not even an open-minded audience. She wanted to prove to herself one last time that she could conquer an audience, no matter how indifferent, no matter how bone-headed. Then, once she'd proved to herself that she still had what it takes, she wouldn't ever need or try to prove it again.'

'So is that why she gave the guitar away, because she had no more use for it?'

'She gave the guitar away?'

The news only hits him slowly, like a tower block being demolished, collapsing in stages into a rising cloud of debris.

'Sure,' said Kate.

'She gave away her guitar,' he repeats. 'Are you sure? The flesh guitar? The one that looks like it's alive?'

'That's the one.'

This time he screams with anguish.

'Do you know what that guitar is worth?' he says. 'You could name your price. You could just think of a number and triple it. And if only I'd been here she could have given it to ME!'

Kate isn't terribly sympathetic.

'You can't be sure of that,' she says. 'Besides, I thought it was quite ugly actually.'

'Ugly,' Bob says despairingly, knowing that it is his destiny to remain misunderstood.

'She gave it to a good-looking boy,' Kate says. 'Besides, you don't even play guitar.'

'That's not the point,' Bob says.

'Anyway, I'm sure that real guitar playing comes from the soul not the instrument.'

'You know,' says Bob, 'you're learning fast.'

Kate nods. 'It's too bad,' she says. 'I thought Jenny Slade was really inspiring, a real role model.'

The BIG thought occurs to them both simultaneously, unfolding like a gaudy flower, but Kate is the first to speak. 'You don't think I'm too old to start learning the guitar, do you?'

'You don't look so old to me,' Bob says.

'I could take lessons,' she enthuses. 'I could practise really intensively, learn my scales, my riffs, my runs, get my chops together.'

'For sure,' says Bob.

'And you could fill me in on the theory.'

'I definitely could,' says Bob.

'I'll need to surround myself with some sympathetic musicians,' Kate says, 'and I'll have to get some stage outfits and publicity photographs and an agent and a record company, and maybe a personal trainer. And a guitar, naturally. And some amplification. And a repertoire. But, of course, what I really need are fans.'

'Don't worry,' says Bob. 'You've already got one of those.'

The sleeping drunk wakes again, lifts an invisible glass and yells, 'Here's to Jenny Slade!'

Bob and Kate do not join in with this toast.

'Where is she now?' the drunk asks. 'Where's she gone, to what godforsaken region? What's she thinking? Is she alone? Is she feeling suicidal? Is she all played out? Is the rest silence?'

There are now tears in his eyes, saliva drooling down his beard.

'One thing's for sure,' he adds. 'We shall not hear her like again.'

'Oh, I don't know about that,' says Bob.

TRASHED CHOIRS

Imagine a cathedral of sorts; an endless chain of arches, some round, some pointed, some four-centred, some ogee. Imagine them in series, a complex, rhythmical arrangement that cuts and curves and zigzags through space like a maze or the framework for a house of mirrors. And imagine them rising, stacked high in irregular storeys, one row on top of another, reaching up to a great and distant height, the upper levels scarcely visible, disappearing in haze or smoke, mounting up and forming an enclosure that is both labyrinth and coliseum. Every arch is open. There are no doors, no walls, no stained glass. And though the principle may be essentially Gothic, there's also something digital, something computer generated about the structure. The stone has a metallic sheen and in places it seems to be dissolving, pixilating like molten polystyrene.

Imagine further that suspended on wires from the apex of each arch is an electric guitar, each fitted with a radio system and connected to unseen banks of amplification. There are countless instruments, wildly varied; all makes, all models, some pristine and glittering, some wrecked, the basic and the customized, the de luxe and the workmanlike, all hanging in suspended, unplayed animation.

Slowly, somewhere off stage, further off than the ear can hear, doors are opened. The stable system within the 'cathedral' is disturbed. Air begins to move through the arches, through the openings. It is a soft, benign motion. The thick, contained air turns, becomes more intricately enfolded. The wires holding the guitars sway and creak.

The movement of air grows and builds, swirling the dust, chafing the stonework. It becomes a wind, strong and mobile and threatening. But what is there to threaten? The architecture is beleaguered, yet still, only the guitars, tautly suspended, can move in time to the deep eddies and gusts of air.

At first the sounds are minimal, mere background quiver and string flutter, or an open tuned twelve string will suddenly be shaken into harmonic life, to give a safe, cascading, multi-voiced chord that seeps into space; the gentle singing of aeolean harps.

Other guitar voices respond; low bass growls, jangling treble. Guitar bodies tremble in the draughts, are raised and dropped. There is the loose twang of swaying whammy bars, the mechanical noises of bridges slipping, of strings unsettling in their courses.

Then an immense gust of air hoiks a guitar through space, a red sparkle double neck, and rams its body against the curving top of an arch, the strings scrape against stone to create stark, chromatic tonalities.

Invisible hands pump up the volume of both wind and guitars, a gale starts to blow through the myriad open-mouthed arches. The instruments are convulsed and battered into new, undreamed-of life. The wind has moved beyond technique, has become an agent of creative rage that sears and yelps from every unseen place, edging towards physical destruction. Invisible hands, ruined choirs, strings planed and shaved by the razored air. A hollow-bodied baritone guitar snaps like firewood against the masonry of a supporting stone column.

Finally there is only a howling, a wail and squalling of wind and feedback, fused, fierce, alarmingly articulate. Weather and electricity play more eloquently than any group of musicians ever did.

And Jenny Slade runs into the maelstrom, empty-handed and unfettered. She finds herself overarched and overwhelmed, a mute matchstick figure beneath the traceried canopy of noise and stone. She is buffeted by the rage of air and sound, yet she remains untouched, the unmoved mover, calm in her eyes. The air cracks, thunder and lightning, cloud bursts of electricity, a tasty cocktail. Spheres of blue energy bounce towards her like footballs. Jenny waits quietly, knows just when the power will come.

Lightning strikes. The electricity hits her, precise and certain, shoots through her veins, along the neural pathways, hammers the pleasure and pain centres. She experiences ecstasy and oblivion. Jenny Slade finally locates the electrical mainline, feels like she's being bounced right out of her body, feels as if she's being finally freed from the tyranny of her dreams and fantasies, from guitars and amps, from performance and audience, being liberated from time and space. A smile cracks her face. This is as good as it gets.